HALF A CHANCE

BY

FREDERIC STEWART ISHAM

Half A Chance

CHAPTER I

MR. GILLETT'S CHARGE

"By all means, m'deah, let's go down between decks and have a look at them."

"Of course, if you wish, Sir Charles, although--Do you think we shall be edified, Mr. Gillett?"

"That depends, m'lady,"--and the speaker, a man with official manners and ferret-like eyes, shifted from one foot to another,--"on what degree, or particular class of criminal your ladyship would be interested in," he added. "If in the ordinary category of skittle sharper or thimblerigger," with a suspicion of mild scorn, "then I do not imagine your ladyship would find much attraction in the present cargo. But, on the other hand," in a livelier tone, "if your ladyship has any curiosity, or shall we say, a psychological bent, regarding the real out-and-outer, the excursion should be to your liking. For," rubbing his hands, "a properer lot of cutthroats and bad magsmen, it has never been my privilege to escort across the equator; and this is my sixth trip to Australia!"

"How interesting! How very interesting!" The lady's voice floated languidly. "Sir Charles is quite right. We must really go down. At any rate, it will be a change, after having been shut up so long in that terrible state-room."

"One moment, m'lady! There's a little formality that must be observed first."

"Formality?" And the lady, who was of portly appearance and uncertain age, gazed from the speaker standing deferentially before her, to a man of size, weight and importance seated in a comfortable chair at her side. "What does he mean, Sir Charles?"

"Regulations, m'lady--m'lord!" was the answer. "No one allowed on the prisoners' deck without the captain's permission. There he is now."

"Then be good enough to beckon to him!" said the lady.

But this Mr. Gillett, agent of the police, discreetly declined to do; Captain Macpherson was a man not to be beckoned to by any one; much less by him. As he stood squarely in the center of the ship, he looked like a mariner capable of commanding his boat and all the people aboard; indeed, some of the characteristics of his vessel seemed to have entered into his own make-up; the man matched the craft. Broad-nosed, wide of beam, big, massive, obstinate-looking, the Lord Nelson plowed aggressively through the seas. With every square sail tugging hard at her sturdy masts, she smote and over-rode the waves, and, beating them down, maintained an unvarying, stubborn poise. But although she refused to vacillate or shuffle to the wooing efforts of the uneasy waters, she progressed not without noise and pother; foamed and fumed mightily at the bow and left behind her a wake, receding almost as far as the eyes might reach. Captain Macpherson looked after the bubbles, cast his glance aloft at the bulging patches of white, and then condescended to observe the agent of the police who had silently approached.

"Sir Charles and lady, and Sir Charles' party have expressed, Captain Macpherson, the desire to obtain permission to visit the prisoners' deck."

Captain Macpherson looked toward Sir Charles and his lady, the other passengers lounging around them, a little girl, at the rail, her hair, blown windward, a splash of gold against the blue sky. "What for?" said the skipper bruskly.

"To have a look at the convicts, I suppose."

"What good'll that do them?" growled the commander. "Idle curiosity, that's what I call it. Well, go along. Only, I'll hold you accountable, and bear this in your mind, no tracts!"

"I don't think," replied Mr. Gillett with some asperity, "you need be apprehensive on that score, Captain Macpherson. Sir Charles and m'lady are not that sort."

"Well, keep them away from the bars. The weather has nae improved the tempers of a few of the rapscallions, and they'd like naught better than a chance for their claws."

"Thanks for the permission, and," a little stiffly, "the admonition, which latter," turning away, "a man whose lifelong profession has been dealing with convicts is most likely to stand in need of and heed."

Captain Macpherson frowned, stumped the other way, then looked once more aloft, and, by the exercise of that ingenuity peculiarly his own, found new tasks for the sailors. Aboard any ship, especially a ship of this character, it was his theory and practice that discipline could not be too strictly maintained and the men on the Lord Nelson knew no idle moments.

"May I go, too?"

The child with the golden hair desisted in her occupation of watching the flying-fish and other real-winged creatures, and, leaving the rail, walked toward the group that was about to follow Mr. Gillett. She was a very beautiful girl of ten or eleven; slim, delicately fashioned, of a definite proud type. But although she held herself erect, in an unconscious patrician sort of way, there was, also, about her something wayward and different from the conventional, aristocratic set. The disordered golden hair proclaimed it, while in the depths of the fine, blue eyes manifold changing lights told of a capriciousness out of the pale of a stiffly decorous and well-contained caste.

"May I go, too, aunt?" she repeated.

"Why, of course!" interposed a blasé, cynical-appearing young man who had just emerged from the cabin. "Don't know where she wants to go, or what she wants to do; but don't say she can't; really you mustn't, now."

"Well, since you insist on spoiling her, Lord Ronsdale--"

He twisted a blond mustache which adorned a handsome face that bore many marks of what is called experience of the world. "Couldn't do that! Besides, Jocelyn and I are great chums, don't you know. We're going to be married some day when she grows up."

"Are we?" said the child. "The man I marry must be very big and strong, and must not have light hair."

Lord Ronsdale laughed tolerantly.

"Plenty of time for you to change your mind, don't you know. Meanwhile, I'll not despair. Faint heart, and so on. But," turning to Sir Charles, "where is it she 'wants to go?'"

"To see the convicts."

"Convicts? Ah!" He spoke rather more quickly than usual, with accent sharper.

"You didn't know who your neighbors were going to be when you decided so suddenly to accompany us?"

"No." His voice had a metallic sound.

Sir Charles addressed Mr. Gillett. "Tell us something more definite about your charges whom we are going to inspect. Meant to have found out earlier in the voyage, but been so jolly seasick, what with one gale after another, I for one, until now, haven't much cared whether we had Claude Duval and

Dick Turpin themselves for neighbors, or whether we all went straight to Davy Jones' locker together. A bad lot, you have already informed us! But how bad?"

"Well, we haven't exactly M. Duval or Mr. Turpin in the pen, but we've one or two others almost as celebrated in their way. There's Billy Burke, as desperate a cracksman as the country can produce, with," complacently, "a record second to none in his class. He"--and Mr. Gillett, with considerable zest entered into the details of Mr. Burke's eventful and rapacious career. "Then there's the ''Frisco Pet,' or the 'Pride of Golden Gate,' as some of the sporting papers call him."

"The 'Frisco Pet!" Lord Ronsdale started; his color slightly changed; his lashes drooped over his cold eyes. "He is on board this vessel?"

"Yes; you remember him, my Lord, I dare say?"

"In common with many others," shortly.

"Many of the gentry and titled classes did honor him with their attention, I believe."

"Why," asked Jocelyn, whose blue eyes were fastened very intently on the face of the police agent, "did they call him such a funny name, the 'Frisco Pet?"

"Because he's a yankee bruiser, prize-fighter, or was, before the drink got him," explained Mr. Gillett. "And originally, I believe, he hailed from the land of the free. Some one brought him to London, found out about his 'talents' and put him in training. He was a low, ignorant sailor; could scarcely write his own name; but he had biceps and a thick head. Didn't know when he was whipped. I can see him yet, as he used to look, with his giant shoulders and his swagger as he stepped into the ring. There was no nonsense about him--or his fist; could break a board with that. And how the shouts used to go up; 'the pet!' 'a quid on the pet!' 'ten bob on the stars and stripes!' meaning the costume he wore. Oh, he was a favorite in Camden Town! But one night he failed them; met some friends from the forecastle of a Yankee trader that had dropped down the Thames. Went into the ring with a stagger added to the swagger. Well, they took him out unconscious; never was a man worse punished. He never got back to the sawdust, and the sporting gentlemen lost a bright and shining light."

"Broke his heart, I suppose," observed Sir Charles.

"How could that break his heart?" asked the child wonderingly. "I thought when people had their hearts broken--"

"Jocelyn, don't interrupt!" said the wife of Sir Charles. "Although," to her husband, in a lower tone, "I must confess these details a little tiresome!"

"Not a bit!" Sir Charles' voice rose in lively protest. "I remember out in Australia reading about the fellow in the sporting papers from home, and wondering what had become of him. So that was it? Go on, Mr. Gillett! With your permission, m'love!"

The police agent proceeded. "After that it was a case of the rum and the toss-pots, and when he was three sheets in the wind, look out for squalls! He got put in quad, broke out, overpowered and nearly killed two guards. Took to various means of livelihood, until they got him again. Trouble in prison; transferred to the solitary with a little punishment thrown in for a reminder. When he got out of limbo again, he lived in bad company, in one of the tunnels near the Adelphi; hard place for the police to rout a cove from. Then followed a series of rough bungling jobs he was supposed to have been mixed up in. At any rate, he got the credit. More hazards than loot! He had too heavy fingers for anything fine; but he made it quite interesting for the police, quite interesting! So much so, he attracted me, and I concluded to take a hand, to direct the campaign against him, as it were."

Mr. Gillett paused; obviously in his case egotism allied to enthusiasm made his duties a pleasure; he seemed now briefly commending himself in his own mind. "Up to this time," he resumed, "our friend, the ex-pugilist, had never actually killed any one, but soon after I engaged myself to look after him, word was brought to the department that a poor woman had been murdered, a cheap music-hall dancer. She had seen better days, however."

Lord Ronsdale, who had been looking away, yawned, as if finding the police agent "wordy," then strolled to the rail.

"Suspicion pointed strongly in his direction; and we got him after a struggle. It was a hard fight, without a referee, and maybe we used him a little rough, but we had to. Then Dandy Joe was brought in. Joe's a plain, mean little gambler and race-track follower, with courage not big enough for broad operations. But he had a wide knowledge of what we term the thieves' catacombs, and, well, he 'peached' on the big fellow. Gave testimony that was of great service to the prosecution. The case seemed clear enough; there was some sort of contrary evidence put in, but it didn't amount to anything. His record was against him and he got a heavy sentence, with death as a penalty, if he ever sets foot in England again."

"What," asked Mr. Gillett's youngest listener, "is 'peached'?"

"In school-girl parlance, it is, I believe, to 'tell on' some one."

"You mean a tattle-tale?" scornfully. "I hate them."

"They have their uses," he answered softly. "And I'm rather partial to them, myself. But if you are ready, m'lord--m'lady--"

"Quite! Egad! I'm curious to have a look at the fellow. Used to like to see a good honest set-to myself occasionally, before I became--ahem!--governor!" And rising with alacrity, Sir Charles assisted his lady from her chair. "Coming, Ronsdale?"

"Believe I won't go down," drawled the nobleman at the rail. "Air better up here," he explained.

Sir Charles laughed, got together the other members of his party and all followed Mr. Gillett to a narrow companion way. There a strong iron door stopped their progress, but, taking a key from his pocket the police agent thrust it into a great padlock, gave it a turn, and swung back the barrier. Before them stretched a long aisle; at each end stood a soldier, with musket; on one side were the cells, small, heavily-barred. The closeness of the air was particularly and disagreeably noticeable; here sunlight never entered, and the sullen beating of the waves against the wooden shell was the only sound that disturbed the tomb-like stillness of the place.

One or two of the party looked soberer; the child's eyes were large with awe and wonder; she regarded, not without dread, something moving, a shape, a human form in each terrible little coop. But Mr. Gillett's face shone with livelier emotions; he peered into the cells at his charges with a keen bright gaze that had in it something of the animal tamer's zest for his part.

"Well, how are we all to-day?" he observed in his most animated manner to the guard. "All doing well?"

"Number Six complained of being ill, but I say it's only the dumps. Number Fourteen's been garrulous."

"Garrulous, eh? Not a little flighty?" The guard nodded; Mr. Gillett whispered a few instructions, asked a number of other questions. Meanwhile the child had paused before one of the cells and, fascinated, was gazing within. What was it that held her? the pity of the spectacle? the terror of it? Her blue eyes continued to rest on the convict, a young fellow of no more than one-and-twenty, of magnificent proportions, but with face sodden and brutish. For his part he looked at her, open-mouthed, with an expression of stupid surprise at the sight of the figure so daintily and slenderly fashioned, at the tangles of bright golden hair that seemed to have imprisoned some of the sunshine from above.

"Well, I'm blowed!" he muttered hoarsely. "Where'd you come from? Looks like one o' them bally Christmas dolls had dropped offen some counter in Fleet Street and got in here by mistake!"

A mist sprang to the blue eyes; she held her white, pretty fingers tight against her breast. "It must be terrible--here"--she said falteringly.

The convict laughed harshly. "Hell!" he said laconically.

The child trembled. "I'm sorry," she managed to say.

The fierce dark eyes stared at her. "What for?"

"Because--you have to stay here--"

"Well, I'm--" But this time he apparently found no adequate adjective. "If this ain't the rummiest Christmas doll!"

She put out her hand. "Here's something for you, poor man," she said, as steadily as she could. "It's my King George gold piece, date , and belonged to my father who wore it on his watch chain and who is dead. Perhaps they'll let you buy something with it."

He looked at the hand. "If she ain't stickin' out her duke to me, right through the bars. Blamed if she ain't! Looks like a lily! A bally white lily!" he repeated wonderingly. "One of them kind we wonst run acrost when the Cap. turned us adrift on an island, jest to waller in green grass!"

"Don't you want it?" said the child.

He extended a great, coarse hand hesitatingly, as if half-minded to and half-minded not to touch the white finger-tips.

"You ain't afraid?"

The golden head shook ever so slightly; again the big hand went toward the small one, then suddenly dropped.

"Right this way m'lord--m'lady!" The face of the convict abruptly changed; fury, hatred, a blind instinct to kill were unmistakably revealed in his countenance as he heard the bland voice of the police agent. From the child's hand the gold disk fell and rolled under the wooden slab that served as a couch in the cell.

"Jocelyn!" The expostulating tones of the governor's wife preceded the approach of the party. "What are you doing, child, so near the bars?"

"Good heavens!" Mr. Gillett seized the girl's arm and abruptly drew her away. "My dear little lady!" he said. "Really you don't know the danger you run. And near that cell of all of them!"

"That cell?" observed Sir Charles. "Then that is--"

"The convict I was telling you about! The 'Pet of 'Frisco.' The 'Pride of Golden Gate.'"

CHAPTER II

A MESSAGE TO THE ADMIRALTY

The following night, Captain Macpherson in his cabin, rolled up carefully the chart he had been scanning, deposited it in a copper cylinder and drew from his pocket a small pipe. As he filled and lighted it, exhaling the smoke of the black weed and leaning more comfortably back in his low, swinging chair, the expression of his iron countenance exhibited, in the slightest degree, that solace which comes from the nicotine. Occasionally, however, he would hold his pipe away from his mouth, to pause and listen. The weather had turned nasty again; above, the wind sounded loudly. Now it descended on the ship like a fierce-scolding virago, then rushed on with wild, shrieking dissonance. The Lord Nelson minded not, but continued steadily on her way.

Her captain emptied his pipe, glanced toward his bunk and started to take off his coat. Human nature has its limit; he had passed many sleepless nights and now felt entitled to a brief respite, especially as the chart showed neither reef nor rock anywhere in the neighborhood. But he had only one arm out of the garment when something happened that caused him to change his mind; abruptly hurled to the other end of the cabin, he found himself lying, half-stunned, on the floor. A hubbub of noises filled the air, snappings, crashings, the rending of woodwork.

Captain Macpherson staggered to his feet, and, swaying like a drunken man, stood a few moments holding his hand to his brow. Then his fist clenched and he shook it at the cylinder that had fallen from the table.

"Ye viperous, lying thing!" he cried, and ran from the cabin to the deck.

A single glance told all: two of the ship's giant spars had gone by the board; entangled in her own wreckage, the vessel thumped and pounded with ominous violence against some sunken reef. The full scope of the plight of the once noble ship was plainly made manifest. Though thick streams of scud sped across the sky, the southern moon at the moment looked down between two dark rivulets, and cast its silvery glow like a lime-light, over the spectacle. Captain Macpherson groaned.

"Mr. O'Brien!" he called loudly.

"Aye, aye, sir."

"How long do you give her?"

"Half an hour, sir."

The master shook his head. "She'll nae last that long." And holding to a stanchion, he seemed like a man in a dream.

"Any orders, sir?" asked the chief mate.

Captain Macpherson recovered himself; his tone became once more quick and incisive. "Ye're right; I'm gone daffy. We'll get this business over in a decorous and decent manner. And, Mr. O'Brien--lest I have nae time to speak of it later--should ye get ashore, and ever find yourself in the neighborhood o' Piccadilly, be so gude as to drop into the admiralty office and say Captain Macpherson sends his compliments, and--to the diel with their charts!"

"I'll not forget, sir!" A number of orders followed.

As the chief mate disappeared to execute the commands he had received, the harsh noises of the breaking ship, the seething of the sea about her, the flapping of canvas, like helpless broken wings, was supplemented by a babel of new and terrifying sounds, the screaming and cursing of the convicts below, their blasphemous shrieking to be let out! To this turmoil and uproar were added the frantic appeals and inquiries of the passengers who, more or less dressed, had hurried to the deck and who were now speaking to the master of the ill-starred vessel. He answered them briefly: what could be done, would be done.

"It's a question of the boats, I suppose?" Sir Charles, one of the calmest of the ship's cabin party, asked quickly.

"In ten minutes they'll be ready for the launching with nae lack of water and provision. Get plenty of wraps and greatcoats. It'll be a bit disagreeable, nae doubt, out yon in the wee craft!"

"Wee craft!" The voice of the governor's lady--she was clinging to her husband's arm--rose shrilly. "You surely are not going to send us out there in one of these miserable cockleshells?"

"M'love!" Sir Charles expostulated mildly drawing her closer as he spoke, "it's the only chance, and--" Then to the captain half-apologetically--"She'll meet it with me, as she has met danger before, in the bush, like a true English-woman! But what," indicating the convicts' deck, "what about them? It seems inhuman, yet if they were let out--"

"They must not be!" Lord Ronsdale's metallic voice interposed quickly. "I call upon you, Captain Macpherson, in the name of the women and children--"

"I've thought about that," said Captain Macpherson shortly, and turned to his task.

The boat was soon overhauled, the lockers and water-butt were filled, and the passengers, one by one, set into it. On the whole, at that moment for leaving the ship, their conduct left little room for criticism; one or two of the women who had appeared on the verge of hysterics now restrained audible manifestation of emotion. Sir Charles proved a monument of helpfulness; assisted in placing the women here and there, and extended a helpful hand to Lord Ronsdale, who had become somewhat dazed and inert. Total darkness added to the difficulties of their task, for the moon which until then had shone with much luster now went behind a curtain of cloud. But Captain Macpherson coolly called out by name the men to handle the life-boat, and, with no evidence of disorder, they crowded in, none too soon! As the boat with its human freight hung in readiness for the lowering, the remaining spar of the Lord Nelson fell with a mighty crash.

"Remember the name of your ship, lads!" Captain Macpherson's voice seemed to anticipate a movement of panic among the seamen on deck; if there had been any intention to "rush" the already well-loaded boat, it was stayed. "Mr. Gillett, I'll be troubling ye for the keys to the convicts' deck. Mr. O'Brien, get in and take charge. Steer southeast with a bit of rag; it's your best chance to get picked up. Hold near the ship until the other boat with the crew can come alongside. It's as well to keep company. Are the lines clear? Let her go."

The boat was lowered and at the right moment touched a receding wave. Captain Macpherson waited until the chief officer called out that they were safely away, then gave his last order:

"And now, lads, ye can be lookin' to yourselves!"

They did; the master turned and with some difficulty made his way toward the convicts' cells. Her decks soon deserted, the ship, like a living, writhing thing, seemed to struggle and groan, as if every timber were crying out in vain protest against the tragic consummation. But only an irrevocable voice answered, that of the mocking sea beating harder, the cruel sea, spotted here and there with black patches between which splashes of light revealed the wild waves throwing high their curd in the cold, argent glimmer. One of these illuminating dashes, as if in a spirit of irony, moved toward the ship, almost enveloped it and showed suddenly a number of mad, leaping human figures issuing with horrible cries from one of the hatches.

"The life rafts! Old man said the boats were gone."

"Rafts good enough for the likes of us, eh? Well, he's paid for keeping us down so long. Blime if I don't think Slick Sam killed him."

"The rafts!" Shrieking, calling down maledictions on the captain, they ran about, when suddenly an angry black wave swept the deck; a few went overboard with the hissing crest; several were hurled against the bulwarks, limp, lifeless things, swirled back and forth. One of their number, a big fellow of unusual strength, was shot toward the open companionway leading to the main cabin; as he plunged down, he clutched at and caught the railing. Considerably shaken, dripping with water, he pulled himself together, and, raising a face, sodden and fierce, like a beast brought to bay, he looked around him. The light of one or two swinging lamps that had not yet been shattered revealed dimly the surroundings, the dark leather upholstering, the little tables. Uncertainly the convict paused; then suddenly his eyes brightened; the lustful anticipation of the drunkard who had long been denied shone from his gaze as it rested on a sideboard across the cabin.

"Bottles!" he said, steadying himself. "Rum! Well, I guess there ain't much chance for any of us, and a man's a fool to go to hell thirsty!" He had started toward the sideboard with its bright gleaming ware and its divers and sundry receptacles of spirits and liqueurs, when suddenly his look changed, and his jaw fell.

"What the--" A flow of choice Billingsgate, mingled with the sailor's equally eloquent Golden-Gate, completed the sentence. The convict stood stock-still.

From the door of a state-room at the far end of the cabin a figure appeared. A great shawl draped the small form; the golden hair, a flurry of tangles, floated around it. Clinging to a brass rail that ran along the side of the cabin, she approached, her eyes all alight as if well satisfied with something. Amazed beyond power of action, the man continued to gaze at her, at the tiny feet in the little pink slippers, at something she carried. "By the great horn spoon, the Christmas doll!" he muttered hoarsely. Then forgetting his purpose, the bottles, he lurched quickly toward her.

"Wat you doin' here?" he demanded.

"I slipped out," said the child, holding the rail tighter, as perforce she paused to answer. "I thought it would take only a moment."

"Slipped out?" he repeated.

"Of the life-boat, I mean. It was dark and they didn't see me. I just happened to think, and I had to do it. If I'd told them, they mightn't have let me. It would have been very wicked if I'd gone away and forgotten--don't you think so? And now I'm going back! Only I am afraid I've been longer than I thought I would be. The door of my state-room seemed to stick, and I was a few minutes getting it open."

Beneath disheveled masses of thick dark hair, the brutish face continued to study the fairylike one; for the instant words seemed to fail him. "Do ye mean," he observed, "you come back here for that measly dicky-bird?"

"It isn't 'measly' and it isn't a 'dicky-bird!'" she answered indignantly. "And I'll thank you not to call it that. It's a love-bird, and its name is Dearie!"

"'Dearie'! Ho! Ho!" The ship reeled at a dangerous angle, but the convict appeared not to notice; his voice rose in harsh, irresistible rough merriment. "'Dearie'! And she thanks me not to call it names! It! No bigger'n my thumb! Ho! Ho!" His laughter, strange at such a moment, died abruptly. "Do you know what you've gone and done on account of what's in that cage?" he demanded almost fiercely. "You've got left!"

"Left?" said she blankly, shrinking from him a little. "You don't mean--oh, I thought I would be only a minute! They haven't really gone, and--"

The great fingers closed on her arm. "They've gone and the crew's gone! Both boats are gone!"

"Oh!" The big blue eyes widened on him; an inkling of her plight seemed to come over her; her lips trembled, but she held herself bravely. "You mean--we must drown?"

The thunder of seas breaking on the deck answered; a cascade of water dashed down the companionway and swept round them. The man bent toward the child. "Look a' that! Now ain't ye sorry ye come back?"

"I couldn't leave it to drown!" passionately--"couldn't!--couldn't!"

"Blow me, she's game!" With difficulty he maintained his equilibrium. "See here: maybe there's a chance, if any of them's left to help with the raft. But we've got to git out o' this!"

He passed his hand through her arm, awaited a favorable moment, and then, making a dash for the stairs, drew her, as best he might, to the deck. At the head of the companionway, the wind smote them fiercely with sheets of foam, but his strength stood him in good stead, and bracing himself hard, the man managed to maintain his stand; holding the child close to him, he sheltered her somewhat from the full force of the storm. As he cast his glance over the deck, an oath burst from his lips; the convicts had succeeded in launching one of the rafts and leaving the ship by means of it, or else had been carried away by the seas. Of living man, he caught no sight; only a single one of the dead yet remained, sliding about on the slippery planks with the movement of the ship; now to leeward, now rushing in a contrary direction, as if some grotesque spirit of life yet animated the dark, shapeless form.

From wave-washed decks the man's glance turned to the sea; suddenly he started; his eyes straining, he stared hard. "Maybe they've missed you. One of the ship's boats seems headin' this way!"

Her gaze followed his; at intervals through driving spray a small craft could be discerned, not far distant, now riding high on a crest, now vanishing in a black furrow.

"Are they coming back to save us?" asked the child.

The convict did not answer. Could the boat make the ship, could it hope to, in that sea? It was easier getting away than getting back. Besides, the opportunity for a desperate, heroic attempt to come alongside was not to be given her, for scarcely had they caught sight of her, when the stern of the Lord Nelson, now filled with water from the inflow at the bow, began to settle more rapidly. Then came a frightful wrenching and the vessel seemed to break in two.

"Put yer arms round my neck," said the man, stooping.

She put one of them around; with the other held up the cage. He opened the door of the wickerwork prison and a tiny thing flew out. Then he straightened. Both arms were around him now.

"'Fraid?" he whispered hoarsely.

The child shook her head.

An instant he waited, then launched himself forward. Buffeted hither and thither, he made a fierce fight for the rail, reached it, and leaped far out into the seething waters.

CHAPTER III

AN UNAPPRECIATED BOUNTY

In the prime of his belligerent career the Pet of 'Frisco had undergone many fierce contests and withstood some terrible punishments, but never had he undertaken a task calling for greater courage and power of endurance than the one he had this night voluntarily assumed. Dashed about by the seas, he yet managed to keep to the surface; minutes seemed to lengthen into eternity; many times he called out loudly. The arms about his neck relaxed, but he held the child to him. Not for an instant did the temptation come to him to release her that he might the more surely save himself. Overwhelmed again and again by the waves, each time he emerged with her tight against his breast; half-strangled, he continued to fight on. But at length even his dogged obstinacy and determination began to flag; he felt his strength going, when raising his eyes he saw one of the small craft from the lost vessel bearing directly down upon him.

The sight inspired new energy and effort; nearer, nearer, she drew; now she was but a few yards away. Then suddenly the sheet of the life-boat went out and the little sail fluttered like a mad thing, while the men bent with might and main over their ash handles in the endeavor to obey the commands of the chief mate in the stern. But despite skill and strength she was not easy to steer; once she nearly capsized; then eager hands reached over the side. The convict held up the child; a voice--the police agent's--called out that they "had her"; and then the mate broke in with harsh, warning yells.

"Pull port!--quick!--or we're over!" And at once the outreaching arms returned quickly to their task; as the child was drawn in, oars dragged and tugged; the life-boat came slowly about, shipping several barrels of water. At the same time some one made the loosened sheet taut, the canvas caught the gust and the craft gained sufficient headway to enable her to run over, and not be run down by the seas. As she careened and plunged, racing down a frothing dark billow, the convict, relieved of his burden, clung to the lower gunwale. By a desperate effort he drew himself up, when a face vaguely remembered--as part of a bad dream--looked into his, with a dash of surprise.

"Eh?--Gimme a hand--"

The asked-for hand swept suddenly under the one grasping the side of the boat, and shot up sharply. In the darkness and confusion no one saw the act. The convict disappeared, but his half-articulate curses followed.

"The fellow's let go," muttered Lord Ronsdale with a shiver.

At the steering oar the chief mate, hearing the cries of the man, cast a swift glance over his shoulder and hesitated. To bring the boat, half-filled with water, around now, meant inevitable disaster; one experiment of the sort had well-nigh ended in their all being drowned. He knew he was personally responsible for the lives in his charge; and with but an instant in which to decide, he declined to repeat the risk.

"He's probably gone by this time, anyhow," he told himself, and drove on.

The convict, however, was not yet quite "gone"; as the boat receded rapidly from view, becoming smaller and smaller, he continued mechanically to use his arms. But he had as little heart as little strength to go on with the uneven contest.

"He's done me! done me!" he repeated to himself. "And I ain't never goin' to git a chance to fix him," he thought, and looked despairingly at the sky. The dark rushing clouds looked like black demons; the stars they uncovered were bright gleaming dagger points. "Ain't never!--the slob!" And with a flood of almost sobbing invective he let himself go.

But as the waters closed over him and he sank, his hand, reaching blindly out to grip in imagination the foe, touched something round--like a serpent, or an eel. His fingers closed about it--it proved to be a line; he drew himself along, and to his surprise found himself again on the surface, and near a great fragment of wreckage. This he might have discovered earlier, but for the anger and hatred that had blinded him to all save the realization of his inability to wreak vengeance. Now, though he managed to reach the edge of the swaying mass from which the line dangled, he was too weak to draw himself up on the floating timbers. But he did pass a loop beneath his arms, and, thus sustained, he waited for his strength to return. Finally, his mind in a daze, the convict clambered, after repeated efforts, upon the wreckage, fastened the line about him again, and, falling into a saucer-like hollow, he sank into unconsciousness.

The night wore on; he did not move. The sea began to subside; still he lay as if dead. Dawn's rosy lips kissed away the black shadows, touched tenderly the waves' tops, and at length the man stirred. He tried to sit up, but at first could not. Finally he raised himself and looked about him.

No other sign of the vessel than that part of it which had served him so well could he see; this fragment seemed rent from the bow; yes, there was the yellow wooden mermaid bobbing to the waves; but not as of old! Poor cast-out trollop,--now the seas made sport of her who once had held her head so high!

The convict continued to gaze out over the ocean. Far away, a dark fringe broke the sea-line--a suggestion of foliage--an island, or a mirage? Tantalizing, it lay like a shadow, illusive, unattainable as the "forgotten isles." The man staggered to his feet; his garments were torn; his hair hung over his brow. He shook his arms at the island;--this phantasy, this vain, empty vision, he regarded it now as some savage creature might a bone just out of its reach; from his lips vile words fell--to be suddenly hushed. Between him and what he gazed at, along the range of vision, an object on one of the projecting timbers caught his eye. It was very small, but it gleamed like a spark sprung from the embers of the dawn.

"The dicky-bird!" His dried lips tried to laugh. "Ef it ain't the dicky-bird!" The bird looked at him. "Ef that doesn't beat--" but he could not think what it "beat." The bird cocked its head. "Ain't ye afeard o' me?" It gave a feeble chirp. "Well, I'm damned!" said the man, and after this mild expression of his feelings, forgot to curse again. He even began to eye the island with a vague questioning wonder, as if asking himself what means might be thought of that would enable him to reach it; but the problem seemed to be beyond solution. The wreckage, like a great lump, lay supinely on the surface of the water; he could not hope to move it.

The day slowly passed; the sun dried his clothes; once or twice the bird made a sound--a plaintive little tone--and involuntarily the man moved with care, thinking not to frighten it. But caution in that regard seemed unnecessary, for the bird appeared very tame and not at all averse to company.

Toward noon the man began to suffer more acutely from thirst, and drawing out a sailors' oilskin pouch, one of the few possessions he had been allowed by the police to retain, he took from it a piece of tobacco which he began to chew. At the same time he eyed the rest of the contents--half a ship's biscuit, some matches and a mariner's thimble. The biscuit he broke, and threw a few crumbs, where the timbers were dry, near the bird. For a long time it looked at the tiny white morsels; but finally, conquering shyness, hopped from its perch and tentatively approached the banquet. Hours went by; the man chewed; the bird pecked.

That night it rained in real, tropical earnest, and he made a water vessel of his shoe, drank many times, ate a few mouthfuls of biscuit, and then placed the filled receptacle where he had thrown the crumbs. As he did so he found himself wondering if the dawn would reveal his little feathered shipmate or whether it had been swept away by the violence of the rain. The early shafts of day showed him the bird on its perch; it had apparently found shelter from the heavy down-pour beneath some out-jutting timber and seemed no worse for the experience. The man's second glance was in the direction of the island; what he saw brought a sudden exclamation to his lips. The land certainly seemed much nearer; some current was sweeping them toward it slowly, but irresistibly. The 'Frisco Pet swore joyfully; his eyes shone. "I may do him yet!" he muttered. The bird chirped; he looked at it. "Breakfast, eh?" he said and tossed a few more crumbs near the shoe.

The second day on the floating bow, he brooded a great deal; the sharper pangs of hunger assailed him; he grew desperately impatient, the distance to the island decreased so gradually. A breeze from the coveted shore fanned his cheek; he fancied it held them back, and fulminated against it,--the beneficent current,--the providential timbers! A feeling of blind helplessness followed; the sun, beating down fiercely, made him light-headed. Hardly knowing what he did, he drew forth the last little bit of the biscuit, ground it between his teeth and greedily swallowed it. The act seemed to sober him; he raised his big hand to his brow and looked at "Dearie"; through the confusion of his thoughts he felt he had done some despicable thing.

"That weren't fair play, were it now?" he said, looking at the bird. "That ain't like a pal," he repeated. The bird remained silent; he fancied reproach in its bead-like eyes, they seemed to bore into him. "And you such a small chap, too!" he muttered; then he turned his back on the island, and, with head resting on his elbow, uttered no further complaint.

That second day on the raft seemed much longer than the first; the second night of infinitely greater duration than the preceding one; but dawn revealed the island very near, so near, indeed, the bird made up its mind to try to reach it. It looked at the man for a moment and then flew away. Long he watched it, a little dark spot--now that he could no longer see the ruby on its breast! At length it was lost to sight; swallowed up by the green blur.

The small winged creature gone, the man missed it. "'Peared like 'twas glad to leave such a pal!" he thought regretfully. The floating timbers became well-nigh intolerable; he kept asking himself if he could swim to land, but, knowing his weakness from long fasting, he curbed his impatience. His eyes grew tired with staring at the longed-for spot; he suffered the torments of Tantalus, and finally could endure them no longer. So making his clothes into a bundle, he tied them around his neck and slipped into the water.

Half an hour later found him, prone and exhausted, on the yellow sands. Near-by, tall and stately trees nodded at him; close at hand a great crab regarded him with reflective interest, hesitating between prudence and carnivorous desire. Gluttonous inclination to sample the goods the gods had provided prevailed over caution; it moved quickly forward, when what it had considered only an unexpected and welcome pièce de résistance abruptly got up. The tables were turned; that which came to dine was dined upon; a crushing blow demonstrated the law of the survival of the fittest; the weaker adorned the board. The man tore it to bits, ate it like the famished animal he was. More freely his blood coursed; he looked around; saw other creatures and laughed. There seemed little occasion for any one to starve here; the isle, a beautiful emerald on the breast of the sea, became a fair battle-ground; all he needed was a club and he soon found that.

For a week nothing of moment interrupted the even tenor of his existence; he led the life of a savage and found it to his liking, pounced upon turtles and cooked them, kept his fire going because he had but few matches. Lying before the blaze at night, near a little spring, he told himself that this was better than being behind prison bars; true, he lacked company, but he had known worse solitude--the "solitary." In it, he had lain on the hard stones; here he had soft moss. If only he could reach out and touch those he hated-- the unknown enemy whose face had bent over him a fleeting instant ere he had struck his hand from the gunwale; Dandy Joe and the police agent--if only they, too, were here, the place would have been world enough for him. But then, he felt, the time for the reckoning must come,--it lay somewhere in the certain future. Unconscious fatalist, he nourished the conviction as he nourished the coals of his fire.

Other means to enhance his physical comfort chance afforded him; the fleshpots were supplemented with a beverage, stronger and more welcome than that which bubbled and trickled so musically at his feet. One day a box was washed ashore; a message from the civilized centers to the field of primitive man! On its cover were the words, "Via sailing vessel, Lord Nelson" followed by the address. The convict pried the boards apart and gave a shout. Rum!--and plenty of it!--bottle after bottle, in an overcoat of straw, nestling lovingly one upon another. The man licked his lips; knocked off a neck, drank deep, and then, stopping many times, carried his treasure to his bower.

Day after day turned its page, merged into the past; sometimes, perforce, he got up, and, not a pleasant thing to look at, staggered to the beach with his club. There he would slay some crawling thing from the sea, return with his prize to mingle eating with drinking, until sated with both, he would fall back unconscious among the flowers. But the prolonged indulgence began to have a marked effect on his store; bottle after bottle was tossed off; the empty shells flung aside to the daisies. At length the day came when only two bottles remained in the case, one full pair, sole survivors of the lot. The man took them out, set them up and regarded them; a sense of impending disaster, of imminent tragedy, shivered through his dulled consciousness. He reached for the bottles and fondled them, started to knock the head from one and put it down. Resisting desire, he told himself he would have a look at the beach; the ocean had generously cast one box of well-primed bottles at his feet; perhaps it would repeat its hospitable action and make him once more the recipient of its bounty. The thought buoyed him to the shore; the sea lapped the sand with Lydian whispers, and there, beyond the edge of the soft singing ripples, he saw something that made him rub his dazed eyes.

A box!--a big box!--a box as tall as he was! No paltry dozen or two this time! Perhaps there was whisky, too; and the bubbling stuff the long-necked lords had sometimes pressed upon him in the past, when he had "ousted" his man and put quids in their pockets; or some of that fiery vin--something he had once indulged in with a Johnny Frenchman before he took to the tunnel, when he had been free to swagger through old Leicester Square. Anyhow, he would soon find out, and, rushing through the water, he laid a proprietary hand on the box. But to his disappointment, he could not move it; strong though he was, its great weight defied him. Ingenuity came to his aid, for, after a moment's pondering, he left the box to the sea and made his way back to the forest. When he returned he bore on his shoulder a straight, stout limb which he had wrenched from a tree, and in his hand he carried a great stone. The former became a lever, the latter, a fulcrum; and, by patient exercise of one of the simple principles of physics, he managed, at length, to transfer the large box from ocean to land.

To break it open was his next problem, and no easy one, for the boards were thick, the nails many and formidable. A long time he battered and battered in vain with his rocks, but, after an hour or so, he succeeded in splintering his way through the tough pine. His exertions did not end here; an inner sheeting of tin caused him to frown; more furiously he attacked this with sharp bits of coral, cutting and bruising his hands. Unmindful of pain, he was enabled at length to pull back a portion of the protecting metal and reveal the contents of the packing-case. In his befuddled, half-crazed condition, he had thought only of bottles; what he found proved a different sort of merchandise.

Maddened, he tossed and scattered the contents of the box on the beach. The ocean had deceived him, laughed at him, cheated him. He turned from the shore unsteadily, walked back to his camp and knocked the neck from one of the two remaining bottles. A few hours later, sodden, sottish, he lay without motion, face to the sky. And as he breathed thickly, one bleeding hand still holding the empty bottle, a bird from an overhanging branch looked down upon him: a tiny bird, little bigger than his thumb, that carried a bright, beautiful spot of red on its breast, cocked its head questioningly.

CHAPTER I

THE WHEELS OF JUSTICE

London, in the spring! Sunshine; the Thames agleam with silver ripples, singing as it flows; red sails! Joyous London that has emerged from fogs and basks beneath blue skies! Thoroughfares that give forth a glad hum; wheels singing, too; whips that crack in sprightly arpeggios. On the streets, people, not shadows, who walk with a swing; who really seem to breathe and not slink uncannily by! Eyes that regard you with human expression; faces that seem capable of emotion; figures adorned in keeping with the bright realities of the moment. London; old London young again; grimy, repulsive London now bright, shimmering, beautiful!

In such a London, on such a day, about ten o'clock in the morning, three persons whose appearance distinguished them from the ordinary passers-by, turned into a narrow thoroughfare not far from the Strand.

"Quite worth while going to hear John Steele conduct for his client, I assure you!" observed one, a tall, military-looking man, who walked with a slight limp and carried a cane. "He's a new man, but he's making his mark. When he asked to be admitted to the English bar, he surprised even his examiners. His summing-up in the Doughertie murder case was, I heard his lordship remark, one of the most masterly efforts he ever listened to. Just tore the circumstantial evidence to pieces and freed his man! Besides his profession at the bar, he is an unusually gifted criminologist; takes a strong personal interest in the lowest riffraff; is writing a book, I understand--one of the kind that will throw a new light on the subject."

"Just what is a criminologist?" The speaker, a girl of about eighteen, turned as she lightly asked the question, to glance over her shoulder toward several persons who followed them.

"One who seeks to apply to the criminal the methods of psychology, psychiatry and anthropology," he answered with jesting impressiveness.

She laughed. "But you said this Mr. Steele comes from our part of the world, did you not, Captain Forsythe?"

"So I understand, Miss Jocelyn. Not much of a person to talk about himself, don't you know,"--tentatively stroking an imposing pair of mustaches, tinged with gray,--"but he has mentioned, I believe, living in New Zealand; or was it Australia?"

"Australia?" the cold, metallic tones of the third person, a man of about three-and-thirty, inquired. "Most likely the other place, or we should have heard--"

"True, Lord Ronsdale!" said the other man, pausing before a great door. "But here we are."

"'All ye who enter, etc'" laughed the girl.

"Not if one comes just to 'do' it, you know," was the protesting answer. "Quite the thing to take in the criminal courts!"

"When one is only a sort of country cousin, a colonial, just come to town!" she added, waving a small, daintily-gloved hand to the little group of friends who now approached and joined them. "Captain Forsythe is trying to persuade me it is a legitimate part of our slumming plan to take in murder trials, uncle," she said lightly, addressing the foremost of the new-comers. "Just because it's a fad of his! Speaking of this acquaintance or friend of yours, Mr. Steele,--you are something of a criminologist, too, are you not, Captain Forsythe?"

"Well, every man should have a hobby," returned that individual, "and, although I don't aspire to the long name you call me, I confess to a slight amateur interest."

Lord Ronsdale shrugged his shoulders, as to say, every one to his taste; but the girl laughed.

"Slight?" she repeated. "Would you believe it, aunt"--to a portly lady among those who had approached--"he never misses a murder trial! I believe he likes to watch the poor fellows fighting for their lives, to study their faces, their expressions when they're being sentenced, perhaps, to one of those horrible convict ships!"

"Don't speak of them, my dear Jocelyn!" returned that worthy person, with a shudder. "When I think of the Lord Nelson, and that awful night--"

"You were three days in an open boat before being sighted and picked up, I believe, Lady Wray?" observed Captain Forsythe.

"Three days? Years!" returned the governor's wife. "At least, they seemed so to me! I thought every moment would be our last and goodness knows why it wasn't! How we managed to survive it--"

"Narrow squeak, certainly!" said Lord Ronsdale, his lids lowering slightly. "But all's well that ends well, and--"

"Every one behaved splendidly," interposed Sir Charles. "You," gazing contemplatively at the girl, "were but a child then, Jocelyn."

She did not answer; the beautiful face had abruptly changed; all laughter had gone from the clear blue eyes.

"She is thinking of the convict who saved her!" observed Sir Charles in an explanatory tone to Captain Forsythe. "Quite an interesting episode, 'pon honor! Tell you about it later. Never saw anything finer, or better. And the amazing part of it is, the fellow looked like a brute, had the low, ignorant face of an ex-bruiser. He'd gone to the bad, taken to drink, and committed I don't know how many crimes! Yet that man, the lowest of the low--"

"You must not speak of him that way!" The girl's hands were clasped; the slender, shapely figure was very straight. Her beautiful blue eyes, full of varying lights, flashed, then became dimmed; a suspicion of mist blurred the long, sweeping lashes. "He had a big, noble spark in his soul. And I think of him many, many times!" she repeated, the sweet, gay lips trembling sensitively. "Brave fellow! Brave fellow!" The words fell in a whisper.

"Fortunate fellow, I should say, to be so remembered by you, Miss Jocelyn!" interposed Captain Forsythe. "Eh, Ronsdale?"

"Fortunate, indeed!" the thin lips replied stiffly.

"Pity he should have been drowned though!" Captain Forsythe went on. "He would, I am sure, have made a most interesting study in contrasts!"

She, however, seemed not to hear either compliment--or comment, but stood for a moment as in a reverie. "I am almost sorry I was persuaded to come here to-day," she said at length, thoughtfully. "I don't believe I shall like courts, or," she added, "find them amusing!"

"Nonsense!" Sir Charles laughed. "I have heard his lordship has a pretty sense of humor, and never fails, when opportunity offers, to indulge it."

"Even when sentencing people?"

"Well; there is no need of turning the proceedings into a funeral."

"I don't believe I should laugh at his wit," said the girl. "And is this Mr. John Steele witty, too?"

"Oh, no! Anything irrelevant from any one else wouldn't be allowed by his lordship."

Here Ronsdale lifted his hat. "May happen back this way," he observed. "That is," looking at Jocelyn Wray, "if you don't object?"

"I? Not at all! Of course, it would bore you--a trial! You are so easily bored. Is it the club?"

"No; another engagement. Thank you so much for permission to return for you--very kind. Hope you will find it amusing. Good morning!" And Lord Ronsdale vanished down the narrow way.

The others of the party entered the court room and were shown to the seats that Captain Forsythe had taken particular pains to reserve for them. The case, evidently an interesting one to judge from the number of people present, was in progress as they quietly settled down in their chairs at the back. From the vantage point of a slight eminence they found themselves afforded an excellent and unimpaired view of his lordship, the jury, prisoner, witness and barristers. Presumably the case had reached an acute stage, for even the judge appeared slightly mindful of what was going on, and allowed his glance to stray toward the witness. The latter, a little man, in cheap attire flashily debonnaire if the worse for long service, seemed to experience difficulty in speaking, to hesitate before his words, and, when he did answer, to betray in his tone no great amount of confidence. He looked weary and somewhat crestfallen, as if his will were being broken down, or subjected to a severe strain, the truth being ground out of him by some irresistible process.

"That's John Steele cross-examining now!" Captain Forsythe whispered to the girl. "And that's Dandy Joe, as he's called, one of the police spies, cheap race-track man and so on, in the box. He came to the front in a murder trial quite celebrated in its day, and one I always had my own little theory about. Not that it matters now!" he added with a sigh.

But the girl was listening to another voice, a clear voice, a quiet voice, a voice capable of the strongest varying accents. She looked at the speaker; he held himself with the assurance of one certain of his ground. His shoulders were straight and broad; he stood like an athlete, and, when he moved, it was impossible to be unconscious of a certain physical grace that came from well-trained muscles. He carried his head high, as if from a habit of thought, of looking up, not down, when he turned from the pages of the heavy tomes in his study; his face conveyed an impression of intelligence and intensity; his eyes, dark, deep, searched fully those they rested on.

He had reached a point in his cross-examination where he had almost thoroughly discredited this witness for the prosecution, when turning toward a table to take up a paper, his glance, casually lifting, rested on the distinguished party in the rear of the room, or rather it rested on one of them. Against the dark background, the girl's golden hair was well-calculated to catch the wandering gaze; the flowers in her hat, the great bunch of violets in her dress added insistent alluring bits of color in the dim spot where she sat. Erect as a lily stem, she looked oddly out of place in that large, somber room; there, where the harsh requiem of bruised and broken lives unceasingly sounded, she seemed like some presence typical of spring, wafted thither by mistake. The man continued to regard her. Suddenly he started, and his eyes almost eagerly searched the lovely, proud face.

His back was turned to the judge, who stirred nervously, but waited a fraction of a second before he spoke.

"If the cross-examination is finished--" he began.

John Steele wheeled; his face changed; a smile of singular charm accompanied his answer.

"Your lordship will pardon me; the human mind has its aberrations. At the moment, by a curious psychological turn, a feature of another problem seized me; it was like playing two games of chess at once. Perhaps your honor has experienced the sensation?"

His lordship beamed. "Quite so," he observed unctuously. "I have to confess that once in a great while, although following a case very closely, I have found it possible to consider at the same time whether I would later have port or sherry with my canvasback."

Of course every one smiled; the business of the morning ran on, and John Steele, at length, concluded his cross-examination. "I think, your Lordship, the question of the reliability of this man, as a witness, in this, or--any other case--fully established."

"Any other case?" said his lordship. "We are not trying any other case."

"Not now, your Lordship." John Steele bowed. "I ask your lordship's indulgence for the"--an instant's ironical light gleamed from the dark eyes--"superfluity."

"Witness may go," said his lordship bruskly.

Dandy Joe, a good deal damaged in the world's estimation, stepped down; his erstwhile well-curled mustache of brick-dust hue seemed to droop as he slunk out of the box; he appeared subdued, almost frightened,--quite unlike the jaunty little cockney that had stepped so blithely forth to give his testimony.

The witnesses all heard, John Steele, for the defense, spoke briefly; but his words were well-chosen, his sentences of classic purity. As the girl listened, it seemed to her not strange that Captain Forsythe, as well as others, perhaps, should be drawn hither on occasions when this man appeared. Straight, direct logic characterized the speech from beginning to end; only once did a suggestion of sentiment--curt pity for that gin-besotted thing, the prisoner!--obtrude itself; then it passed so quickly his lordship forgot to intervene, and the effect remained, a flash, illuminating, Rembrandt-like!

Time slipped by; the judge looked at his watch, bethought him of a big silver dish filled with an amber-hued specialty of the Ship and Turtle, and adjourned court. His address interrupted by the exigencies of the moment, John Steele began mechanically to gather up his books; his face that had been marked by the set look of one determined to drive on at his best with a task, now wore a preoccupied expression. The prisoner whined a question; Steele did not answer, and some one bustled the man out. Having brought his volumes together in a little pile, Steele absently separated them again; at the same time Sir Charles and his party walked toward the bench. They were met by his lordship and cordially greeted.

"A privilege, Sir Charles, to meet one we have heard of so often, in the antipodes."

"Thank you. His lordship, Judge Beeson, m'dear, whose decisions--"

"Allow me to congratulate you, sir!" The enthusiastic voice was that of Captain Forsythe, addressing John Steele. "Your cross-examination was masterly; had you been in a certain other case, years ago, when the evidence of that very person on the stand to-day--in the main--convicted a man of murder, I fancy the result then would have been different!"

John Steele seemed not to hear; his eyes were turned toward the beautiful girl. She was standing quite close to him now; he could detect the fragrance of the violets she wore, a fresh sweet smell so welcome in that close, musty atmosphere.

"My niece, your Lordship, Miss Wray."

Steele saw her bow and heard her speak to that august court personage; then as the latter, after further brief talk, hurried away--

"Sir Charles, let me present to you Mr. Steele," said Captain Forsythe. "Lady Wray--"

"Happy to know you, sir," said the governor heartily.

"Miss Jocelyn Wray," added the military man, "who," with a laugh, "experienced some doubts about a visit of this kind being conducive to pleasure!"

John Steele took the small gloved hand she gave him; her eyes were very bright.

"I enjoyed--I don't mean that--I am so glad I came," said the girl. "And heard you!" she added.

He thanked her in a low tone, looking at her hand as he dropped it. "You,-- you are making England your home?" His voice was singularly hesitating!

"Yes." She looked at him a little surprised. "At least, for the present! But how--" she broke off. "I suppose, though, you could tell by my accent. I've lived nearly all my life in Australia, and--"

Sir Charles, interrupting, reminded them of an appointment; the party turned. A slender figure inclined itself very slightly toward John Steele; a voice wished him good morning. The man stood with his hands on his books; it did not occur to him to accompany her to the door. Suddenly he looked over his shoulder; at the threshold, she, too, had turned her head. An instant their glances met; the next, she was gone.

CHAPTER II

AT THE OPERA

When John Steele left the court toward the end of the day, he held his head as a man who thinks deeply. From the door he directed his steps toward Charing Cross. But only to wheel abruptly, and retrace his way. He was not an absent-minded man, yet he had been striding unconsciously not toward his customary destination at that hour, the several chambers at once his office and his home. For a moment the strong face of the man relaxed, as if in amusement at his own remissness; gradually however, it once more resumed its expression of musing thoughtfulness. The stream of human beings, in the main, flowed toward him; he breasted the current as he had for many evenings, only this night he did not look into the faces of these, his neighbors; the great city's concourse of atoms swept unmeaningly by.

Turning into a narrow way, not far from the embankment, he stopped before the door of a solid-looking brick building, let himself in, and made his way up-stairs. On the third floor he applied another and smaller key to another lock and, from a hall, entered a large apartment, noteworthy for its handsome array of books that reached from floor to ceiling wherever there was shelf space. Most of these volumes were soberly bound in conventional legal garb but others in elegant, more gracious array, congregated, a little cosmopolitan community, in a section by themselves.

Passing through this apartment, John Steele stepped into that adjoining, the sitting-and dining-room. The small table had already been set; the sun's dying rays that shot through the window revealed snowy linen, brightly gleaming silver and a number of papers and letters. They showed, also, a large cage with a small bird that chirped as the man came in; John Steele looked at it a moment, walked to a mirror and looked at himself. Long the deep eyes studied the firm resolute face; they seemed endeavoring to gaze beyond it; but the present visage, like a shadow, waved before him. The man's expression became inscrutable; stepping to the window, he gazed out on the Thames. A purplish glimmer lent enchantment to the noble stream; it may be as he looked upon it, his thoughts flowed with the river, past dilapidated structures, between whispering reeds on green banks, to the sea!

A discreet rapping at the door, followed by the appearance of a round-faced little man, with a tray, interrupted further contemplation or reverie on John Steele's part. Seating himself at the table, he responded negatively to the servant's inquiry if "anythink" else would be required, and when the man had withdrawn, mechanically turned to his letters and to his simple evening repast. He ate with no great evidence of appetite, soon brushed the missives, half-read, aside, and pushed back his chair.

Lighting a pipe he picked up one of the papers, and for some moments his attention seemed fairly divided between a casual inspection of the light arabesques that ascended in clouds from his lips and the heavy-looking columns of the morning sheet. Suddenly, however, the latter dissipated his further concern in his pipe; he put it down and spread out the big paper in both hands. Amid voluminous wastes of type an item, in the court and society column, had caught his eye:

"Sir Charles and Lady Wray, who are intending henceforth to reside in England, have returned to the stately Wray mansion in Piccadilly, where they will be for the season. Our well-known Governor and his Lady are accompanied by their niece, the beautiful and accomplished Miss Jocelyn Wray, only child of Sir Charles' younger brother, the late Honorable Mr. Richard Wray, whose estate included enormous holdings in Australia as well as several thousand acres in Devonshire. This charming young colonial has already captivated London society."

John Steele read carefully this bit of news, and then re-read it; he even found himself guilty of perusing all the other paragraphs; the comings and goings, the fine doings! They related to a world he had thought little about; a world within the world; just as the people who lived in tunnels and dark passages constituted another world within the world. Her name danced in illustrious company; here were dukes and earls and viscounts; a sprinkling of the foreign element: begums, emirs, the nation's guests. He saw, also, "Sir Charles, Lady Wray and Miss Wray" among the long list of box-holders for that night at the opera, a gala occasion, commanded by royalty for the entertainment of royalty, and, incidentally, of certain barbarian personages who had come across the seas to be diplomatically coddled and fed.

Folding his newspaper, John Steele turned to his legal papers; strove to replace idleness by industry; but the spirit of work failed to respond. He looked at his watch, rang sharply a bell.

"Put out my clothes," he said to the servant who appeared with a lamp, "and have a cab at the door."

The opera had already begun, but pandemonium still reigned about the box-office, and it was half an hour before John Steele succeeded in reaching the little aperture, with a request for anything that chanced to be left down-stairs. Armed with a bit of pasteboard, Steele was stopped as he was about to enter. A thunder of applause from within, indicating that the first act had come to an end, was followed by the usual egress of black and white figures, impatient for cigarettes and light lobby gossip.

"Divine, eh? The opera, I mean!" A voice accosted John Steele, and, turning, he beheld a familiar face with black whiskers, that of Captain Forsythe. "This is somewhat different from the morning's environment?"

"Yes," said the other. "But your first question," with a smile, "I'm afraid I can't answer. I've just come; and, if I hadn't--well, I'm no judge of music."

"Then you must look as if you were!" laughed the captain frankly. "Don't know one jolly note from another, but, for goodness' sake, don't betray me. Just been discussing trills and pizzicatos with Lady Wray."

For a few moments they continued their talk; chance had made them known to each other some time before, and Captain Forsythe had improved every opportunity to become better acquainted with one for whom he entertained a frank admiration. Steele's reserve, however, was not easily penetrated; he accepted and repaid the other's advances with uniform courtesy but Forsythe could not flatter himself the acquaintance had progressed greatly since their first meeting.

A bell sounded; John Steele, excusing himself, entered the auditorium and was shown to his seat. It proved excellently located, and, looking around, he found himself afforded a comprehensive view of a spectacle brilliant and dazzling. Boxes shone with brave hues; gems gleamed over-plentifully; here and there, accentuating the picture, the gorgeous colors of some eastern prince stood out like the brighter bits in a kaleidoscope. Steele's glance swept over royalty, rank and condition. It took in persons who were more than persons--personages; it passed over the impassive face of a dark ameer who looked as if he might have stepped from one of the pages of The Arabian Nights, and lingered on a box a little farther to one side. Here were seated Sir Charles and his wife and party; and among them he could discern the features of Jocelyn Wray--not plainly, she was so far away! Only her golden hair appeared distinct amid many tints.

The curtain went up at last; the music began; melodies that seemed born in the springtime succeeded one another. Perennial in freshness, theme followed theme; what joy, what gladness; what merriment, what madness! John Steele, in the main, kept his attention directed toward the stage; once or twice he glanced quickly aside and upward; now in the dimness, however, the people in the boxes conveyed only a vague shadowy impression. How long was the act; how short? It came to a sudden end; after applause and bravos, men again got up and walked out; he, too, left his seat and strolled toward the back.

"Mr. Steele! One moment!" He found himself once more addressed by the good-humored Captain Forsythe. "Behold in me a Mercury, committed to an imperative mission. You are commanded to appear--not in the royal box--but in Sir Charles'."

"Sir Charles Wray's?" John Steele regarded the speaker quickly.

"Yes," laughed the other. "You see I happened to mention I had seen you. 'Why didn't you bring him with you to the box?' queried Sir Charles. He, by the by, went in for law himself, before he became governor. 'Only had time to shake hands this morning!' 'Yes, why didn't you?' spoke up Miss Jocelyn. 'You command me to bring him?' I inquired. 'By all means!' she laughed, 'I command.' So here I am."

John Steele did not answer, but Captain Forsythe, without waiting for a reply, turned and started up the broad stairway. The other, after a moment's hesitation, followed, duly entered one of the larger boxes, spoke to Sir Charles and his wife and returned the bow of their niece. Amid varied platitudes Steele's glance turned oftenest to the girl. She was dressed in white; a snowy boa drooped from the slender bare shoulders as if it might any moment slip off; a string of pearls, each one with a pearl of pure light in the center, clasped her throat. In her eyes the brightness seemed to sing of dancing cadenzas; her lips, slightly parted, wore the faint suggestion of a smile, as if some canticle or clear cadence had just trembled from them. The small shoe that peeped from beneath silken folds tapped softly to rhythms yet lingering; on her cheeks two small roses unfolded their glad petals.

"I trust Captain Forsythe did not repeat that absurd remark of mine?" she observed lightly, when John Steele, after a few moments' general talk, found himself somehow by her side.

"About 'commanding'?"

"So he did?" she answered gaily. "He told me he was going to. It is like him; he poses as a bel esprit. Stupid, was it not?"

He answered a word in the negative; the girl smiled; where other men would press the opportunity for a compliment he apparently found no opening.

She waved her hand to the seat next to her, and as he sat down--"Isn't it splendid!" irrelevantly.

"The spectacle, or the opera?" he asked slowly, looking into blue eyes.

"It was the opera I meant. I suppose the spectacle is very grand; but," enthusiastically, "it was the music I was thinking of--how it grips one! Tell me what you think of The Barber, Mr. Steele."

"I'm afraid my views wouldn't be very interesting," he answered. "I know nothing whatever about music."

"Nothing?" Her eyes widened a little; in her accent was mild wonder.

He looked down at the shimmering white folds near his feet. "In earlier days my environment was not exactly a musical one."

"No? I suppose you were engaged in more practical concerns?"

He did not answer directly. "Perhaps you wouldn't mind telling me something about Rossini's music, Miss Wray?"

"I tell you?" Her light silvery laugh rang out. "And Captain Forsythe has only been telling me--all of us--that you were one of the best informed men he had ever met."

"You see how wrong he was!"

"Quite!" The blue eyes regarded him sidewise. He, the keen, strong man, so assured, so invincible in the court room, sat most humbly by her side, confessing his ignorance, want of knowledge about something every school-girl is mistress of! "Or, perhaps, it is because your world is so different from mine! Music, laughter, the traditions of Italian bel canto, you have no room for them, they are too light, too trifling. You are above them," poising her fair head a little higher.

"Perhaps they have been above me," he answered, his tone unconsciously taking an accent of gaiety from the lightness of hers.

The abrupt appearance of the musicians and the dissonances attendant on tuning, interrupted her response; Steele rose and was about to take his departure, when Sir Charles intervened.

"Why don't you stay?" he asked, with true colonial heartiness. "Plenty of room! Unless you've a better place! Two vacant chairs!"

John Steele looked around; he saw three vacant chairs and took one, a little aside and slightly behind the young girl, while the governor's wife, who had moved from the front at the conclusion of the previous act, now returned to her place, next her niece. During the act, some one came in and took a seat in the background; if Steele heard, he did not look around. His gaze remained fastened on the stage; between him and it--or them, art's gaily attired illusions!--a tress of golden hair sometimes intervened, but he did not move. Through threads like woven flashes of light he regarded the scene of the poet's fantasy. Did they make her a part of it,--did they seem to the man the fantasy's intangible medium, its imagery? Threads of gold, threads of melody! He saw the former, heard the latter. They rose and fell wilfully, capriciously, with many an airy and fanciful turn. The man leaned his head on his hand; a clear strain died like a filament of purest metal gently broken. She breathed a little quicker; leaned farther forward; now her slender figure obtruded slightly between him and the performers. He seemed content with a partial view of the stage, and so remained until the curtain went down. The girl turned; in her eyes was a question.

"Beautiful!" said the man, looking at her.

"Charming! What colorature! And the bravura!" Captain Forsythe applauded vigorously.

"You've never met Lord Ronsdale, I believe, Mr. Steele?" Sir Charles' voice, close to his ear, inquired.

"Lord Ronsdale!" John Steele looked perfunctorily around toward the back of the box and saw there a face faintly illumined in the light from the stage: a cynical face, white, mask-like. Had his own features not been set from the partial glow that sifted upward, the sudden emotion that swept Steele's countenance would have been observed. A sound escaped his lips; was drowned, however, in a renewed outbreak of applause. The diva came tripping out once more, the others, too--bowing, smiling--recipients of flowers. John Steele's hand had gripped his knee tightly; he was no longer aware of the stage, the people, even Jocelyn Wray. The girl's attention had again centered on the actors; she with the others had been oblivious to the glint of his eyes, the hard, set expression of his features.

"Old friend, don't you know," went on the voice of Sir Charles when this second tumult of applause had subsided. "Had one rare adventure together. One of the kind that cements a man to you."

As he spoke, the light in the theater flared up; John Steele, no longer hesitating, uncertain, rose; his face had regained its composure. He regarded the slender, aristocratic figure of the nobleman in the background; faultlessly dressed, Lord Ronsdale carried himself with his habitual languid air of assurance. The two bowed; the stony glance of the lord met the impassive one of the man. Then a puzzled look came into the nobleman's eyes; he gazed at Steele more closely; his glance cleared.

"Thought for an instant I'd seen you somewhere before, b'Jove!" he drawled in his metallic tone. "But, of course, I haven't. Never forget a face, don't you know."

"I may not say so much, may not have the diplomat's gift of always remembering people to the extent your lordship possesses it, but I am equally certain I have never before enjoyed the honor of being presented to your lordship!" said John Steele. The words were punctiliously spoken, his accents as cold as the other's. An infinitesimal trace of constraint seemed to have crept into the box; Steele turned and holding out his hand, thanked Sir Charles and his wife for their courtesy.

Jocelyn Wray gazed around. "You are leaving before the last act?" she said with an accent of surprise.

He looked down at her. "Not through preference!"

"Ah!" she laughed. "Business before--music, of course!"

"Our day at home, Mr. Steele, is Thursday," put in the governor's lady, majestically gracious.

"And you'll meet a lot of learned people only too glad to talk about music," added the young girl in a light tone. "That is, if you were sincere in your request for knowledge, and care to profit by the opportunity?"

His face, which had been contained, impassive, now betrayed in the slightest degree an expression of irresolution. Her quick look caught it, became more whimsical; he seemed actually, for an instant, asking himself if he should come. She laughed ever so slightly; the experience was novel; who before had ever weighed the pros and cons when extended this privilege? Then, the next moment, the blue eyes lost some of their mirth; perhaps his manner made her feel the frank informality she had unconsciously been guilty of; she regarded him more coldly.

"Thank you," he said. "You are very good. I shall be most glad."

And bowing to her and to the others he once more turned; as he passed Lord Ronadsle, the eyes of the two men again met; those of the nobleman suddenly dilated and he started.

"B'Jove!" he exclaimed, his gaze following the retreating figure.

"What is it?" Sir Charles looked around. "Recall where you thought you saw him?"

Lord Ronsdale did not at once answer and Sir Charles repeated his question; the nobleman mechanically raised his hand to his face. "Yes; a mere fugitive resemblance," he answered rather hurriedly. "Some one--you--you never met. Altogether quite a different sort of person, don't you know!" regaining his drawl.

"Well," observed Sir Charles, "fugitive resemblances will happen!"

CHAPTER III

A LESSON IN BOTANY

John Steele was rather late in arriving at the house of Sir Charles Wray in Piccadilly the following Thursday. But nearly every one else was late, and, perhaps knowing the fashionable foible, he had purposely held back to avoid making himself conspicuous by being prompt. The house, his destination, was not unlike other dwellings on that historic thoroughfare; externally it was as monotonous as the average London mansion. The architect had disdained any attempt at ornamentation. As if fearful of being accused of emulating his brother-in-art across the channel, he had put up four walls and laid on a roof; he had given the front wall a slightly outward curve. In so doing, he did not reason why; he was merely following precedent that had created this incomprehensible convexity.

But within, the mansion made a dignified and at the same time a pleasant impression. John Steele, seated at the rear of a spacious room, where he a few moments later found himself among a numerous company, looked around on the old solid furnishings, the heavy rich curtains and those other substantial appurtenances to a fine and stately town house. That funereal atmosphere common to many homes of an ancient period was, however, lacking. The observer felt as if some recent hand, the hand of youth, had been busy hereabouts indulging in light touches that relieved and gladdened the big room. Hues, soft and delicate, met the eye here and there; rugs of fine pattern favored the glance, while tapestries of French workmanship bade it wander amid scenes suggestive of Arcadia. Many found these innovations to their liking; others frowned upon them; but everybody flocked to the house.

The program on the present occasion included a poet and a woman novelist. The former, a Preraphaelite, led his hearers through dim mazes, Hyrcanian wilds. The novelist on the other hand was direct; in following her there seemed no danger of losing the way. At the conclusion of the program proper, an admirer of the poet asked if their young hostess would not play a certain musical something, the theme of one of the bard's effusions, and at once Jocelyn Wray complied. Lord Ronsdale stood sedulously near, turning the leaves; Steele watched the deft hand; it was slim, aristocratic and suggested possibilities in legerdemain.

"An attractive-looking pair!" whispered a woman near John Steele to another of her sex, during a louder passage in the number. "Are they--"

"I don't know; my dear. Perhaps. She's extremely well-off in this world's goods, and he has large properties, but--a diminishing income." She lowered her voice rather abruptly as the cadence came to a pause. The music went on again to its appointed and spirited climax.

"Was formerly in the diplomatic service, I believe;"--the voice also went on--"has strong political aspirations, and, with a wealthy and clever wife--"

"A girl might do worse. He is both cold and capable--an ideal combination for a political career--might become prime minister--with the prestige of his family and hers to--"

John Steele stirred; the whispering ceased. My lord turned the last page; the girl rose and bent for an instant her fair head. And as Steele looked at her, again there came over him--this time, it may be, not without a certain bitterness!--an impression of life and its joys--spring-tide and sunshine, bright, remote!--so remote--for him--

A babel of voices replaced melody; the people got up. A number lingered; many went, after speaking to their hostesses and Sir Charles. John Steele, at the rear, looked at the door leading into the main hall toward the young girl, then stepped across the soft rugs and spoke to her. She answered in the customary manner and others approached. He was about to draw back to leave, when--

"Oh, Mr. Steele," she said, "my uncle wishes to see you before you go. He was saying he had some--"

"Quite right, my dear!" And Sir Charles, who had approached, took John Steele's arm. "Some curious old law books I picked up to-day at a bargain and want your opinion of!" he went on, leading the other into a lofty and restful apartment adjoining, the library. Steele looked around him; his gaze brightened as it rested on the imposing and finely bound volumes.

"You have a superb collection of books," he observed with a sudden quick look at his host.

"Yes; I rather pride myself on my library," said Sir Charles complacently. "Lost a good many of the choicest though," he went on in regretful tones, "some years ago, as I was returning to Australia. A rare lot of law books, a library in themselves, as well as a large collection of the classics, the world's poets and historians, went down with the ill-fated Lord Nelson."

"Ah?" John Steele looked away. "A great mart, London, for fine editions!" he said absently after a pause.

"It is. But here are those I spoke of." And Sir Charles indicated a number of volumes on a large center table. John Steele handled them thoughtfully and for some time his host ran on about them. A choice copy of one of the Elizabethan poets, intruding itself in that august company, then attracted Steele's attention; he picked it up, weighed and caressed it with gentle fingers.

"Who shall measure the influence of--a little parcel like this?" he said at length lightly.

"True." Sir Charles' eye caught the title. "As Portia says: 'It blesseth him that gives and him that takes.' Excellent bit of binding that, too! But," with new zest, "take any interest in rare books of the ring, full of eighteenth century colored prints, and so on?"

"I can't say, at present, that the doings of the ring or the history of pugilists attract me."

"That's because you've never seen an honest, hard-fought battle, perhaps?"

"A flattering designation, I should say, of the spectacle of two brutes disfiguring their already repulsive visages!"

"Two brutes?--disfiguring?"--the drawling voice of Lord Ronsdale who had at that moment stepped in, inquired. "May I ask what the--talk is about?"

Sir Charles turned. "Steele was differing from me about a good, old, honest English sport."

"Sport?" Lord Ronsdale dropped into a chair and helped himself to whisky and soda conveniently near.

"I refer to the ring--its traditions--its chronicles--"

"Ah!" The speaker raised his glass and looked at John Steele. The latter was nonchalantly regarding the pages of a book he yet held; his face was half-turned from the nobleman. The clear-cut, bold profile, the easy, assured carriage, so suggestive of strength, seemed to attract, to compel Lord Ronsdale's attention.

"For my part," went on Sir Charles in a somewhat disappointed tone, "I am one who views with regret the decadence of a great national pastime."

He regarded Ronsdale; the latter set down his glass untasted. "My own opinion," he said crisply; then his face changed; he looked toward the door.

"Well, it's over!" the light tones of Jocelyn Wray interrupted; the girl stood on the threshold, glancing gaily from one to the other. "Did you tell my uncle, Mr. Steele, what you thought of his purchase? I see, while on his favorite subject, he has forgotten to offer you a cigar."

Sir Charles hastened to repair his remissness.

"But how," she went on, "did it go? The program, I mean. Have you forgiven me yet for asking you to come, Mr. Steele?"

"Forgiven?" he repeated. Lord Ronsdale's eyes narrowed on them.

"Confess," she continued, sinking to the arm of a great chair, "you had your misgivings?"

He regarded the supple, slender figure, so airily poised. As she bent forward, he noticed in her hair several flowers shaped like primroses, but light crimson in hue. "What misgivings was it possible to have?" he replied.

"Oh," she replied, "the usual masculine ones! Misgivings, for example, about stepping out of the routine. Routine that makes slaves of men!" with an accent slightly mocking. "And stepping into what? Society! The bugbear of so many men! Poor Society! What flings it has to endure! By the way, did your convict get off?"

"Get off? What--"

"The one you represented--is that the word?--when we were in court."

"Yes; he was acquitted."

"I am glad; somehow you made me feel he was innocent."

"I believed in him," said John Steele.

"And yet the evidence was very strong against him! If some one else had appeared for him--Do you think many innocent people have been--hanged, or sent out of the country, Mr. Steele?" Her eyes looked brighter, her face more earnest now.

"Evidence can play odd caprices."

"Still, your average English juryman is to be depended on!" put in Lord Ronsdale quickly.

"Do you think so?" An instant Steele's eyes rested on the speaker. "No doubt you are right." A sardonic flash seemed to play on the nobleman. "At all events you voice the accepted belief."

"I'm glad you defend, don't prosecute people, Mr. Steele," said the girl irrelevantly.

"A pleasanter task, perhaps!"

"Speaking of sending prisoners out of the country," broke in Sir Charles, "I am not in favor of the penal system myself."

"Rather a simple way of getting rid of undesirables--transportation--it has always seemed to me," dissented Lord Ronsdale.

"Don't they sometimes escape and come back to England?" asked the girl.

"Not apt to, when death for returning stares them in the face," remarked the nobleman.

"Death!" The girl shivered slightly.

John Steele smiled. "The penalty should certainly prove efficacious," he observed lightly.

"Is not such a penalty--for returning, I mean--very severe, Mr. Steele?" asked Jocelyn Wray.

"That," he laughed, "depends somewhat on the point of view, the criminal's, or society's!" His gaze returned to her; the bright bit of color in her hair again seemed to catch and hold his glance. "But," with a sudden change of tone, "will you explain something to me, Miss Wray? Those flowers you wear--surely they are primroses, and yet--"

"Crimson," said the girl. "You find that strange. It is very simple. If you will come with me a moment." She rose, quickly crossed the room to a door at the back, and Steele, following, found himself in a large conservatory that looked out upon an agreeable, if rather restricted, prospect of green garden. Several of the windows of the glass addition were open and the warm sunshine and air entered. A butterfly was fluttering within; in a corner, a bee busied himself buzzing loudly between flowers and sips of saccharine sweetness. Jocelyn Wray stepped in its direction, stooped. The sunlight touched the white neck, where spirals of gold nestled, and fell over her gown in soft, shifting waves.

"You see?" She threw over her shoulder a glance at him; he looked down at primroses, pale yellow; a few near-by were half-red, or spotted with crimson; others, still, were the color of those that nodded in her hair. "You can imagine how it has come about?"

He regarded a great bunch of clustering red roses--the winged marauder hovering noisily over. "I think I can guess. The bees have carried the hue of the roses to them."

"Hue!" cried the girl, with light scorn. "What a prosaic way to express it! Say the soul, the heart's blood. Some of the primroses have yielded only a little; others have been transformed."

"You think, then, some flowers may be much influenced by others?"

"They can't help it," she answered confidently.

"Just as some people," he said in a low tone, "can't help taking into their lives some beautiful hue born of mere casual contact with some one, some time."

"What a poetical sentiment!" she laughed. "Really, it deserves a reward." As he spoke, she plucked a few flowers and held them out in her palm to him; he regarded her merry eyes, the bright tints.

Erect, with well-assured poise, she looked at him; he took one of the flowers, gazed at it, a tiny thing in his own great palm, a tiny, red thing, like a jewel in hue--that reminded him of--what? As through a mist he saw a spark-- where?

"Only one?" she said in the same tone. "You are modest. And you don't even condescend to put it in your coat?"

He did so; in his gaze was a sudden new expression, something so compelling, so different, it held her, almost against her will. He seemed to see her and yet not fully to be aware of her presence; she drew back slightly. The girl's crimson lips parted as with a suspicion of faint wonder; the blue eyes, just a little soberer, were, also, in the least degree, perplexed. The man's breast suddenly stirred; a breath--or was it the merest suggestion of a sigh?--escaped the firm lips. He looked out of the window at the garden, conventional, the arrangement of lines one expected.

When his look returned to her it was the same he had worn when he had first stepped forward to speak with her that afternoon.

"Thank you for the lesson in botany, Miss Wray!" he said easily. "I shall not forget it."

The other primroses fell from her fingers; with a response equally careless if somewhat reserved, she turned and reëntered the library. Lord Ronsdale regarded both quickly; then started, as he caught sight of the flower in John Steele's coat. A frown crossed his face and he looked away to conceal the singularly cold and vindictive gleam that sprang to his eyes.

CHAPTER IV

TIDES VARYING

One evening about a fortnight later Lord Ronsdale, in a dissatisfied frame of mind, strolled along Piccadilly. His face wore a dark look, the expression of one ill-pleased with fortune's late attitude toward him. Plans that he had long cherished seemed to be in some jeopardy; he had begun to flatter himself that the flowery way to all he desired lay before him and that he had but to tread it, when another, as the soothsayers put it, had crossed his path.

A plain man, a man without title! Lord Ronsdale told himself Miss Jocelyn Wray was no better than an arrant coquette, but the next moment questioned this conclusion. Had she not really been a little taken by the fellow? Certainly she seemed not averse to his company; when she willed, and she willed often, she summoned him to her aide. Nor did he now appear reluctant to come at her bidding; self-assertive though he had shown himself to be he obeyed, sans demur, the wave of my lady's little hand. Was it a certain largeness and reserve about him that had awakened her curiosity? From her high social position had she wished merely to test her own power and amuse herself after a light fashion, surely youth's and beauty's privilege?

But whatever the girl's motive, her conduct in the matter reacted on my lord; the fellow was in the way, very much so. How could he himself pay court to her when she frivolously, if only for the moment, preferred this commoner's company? That very afternoon my lord, entering the music-room of the great mansion, had found her at the piano playing for him, her slim fingers moving over the keys to the tune of one of Chopin's nocturnes. He had surprised a steady, eloquent look in the fellow's eye turned on her when she was unconscious of his gaze, a glance the ardency of which there was no mistaking. It had altered at my lord's rather quiet and abrupt appearance, crystallized into an impersonal icy light, colder even than the nobleman's own stony stare. He had, perforce, to endure the other's presence and conversation, an undercurrent to the light talk of the girl who seemed, Lord Ronsdale thought, a little maliciously aware of the constraint between the two men, and not at all put out by it.

What made the situation even more anomalous to Ronsdale and the less patiently to be borne, was that Sir Charles understood and sympathized with his desires and position in the matter. And why not? Ronsdale's father and Sir Charles had been old and close friends; there were reasons that pointed to the match as a suitable one, and Sir Charles, by his general manner and attitude, had long shown he would put no obstacle in the way of the nobleman's suit for the hand of his fair niece. As for Lady Wray, Lord Ronsdale knew that he had in that practical and worldly person a stanch ally of his wishes; these had not become less ardent since he had witnessed the unqualified success of the beautiful colonial girl in London; noted how men, illustrious in various walks of life, grave diplomats, stately ambassadors, were swayed by her light charm and impulsive frankness of youth. And to have her who could have all London at her feet, including his distinguished self, show a predilection, however short-lived and capricious, for--

"Confound the cad! Where did he come from? Who are his family--if he has one!"

Thus ruminating he had drawn near his club, a square, imposing edifice, when a voice out of the darkness caused him abruptly to pause:

"If it isn't 'is lordship!"

The tones expressed surprise, satisfaction; the nobleman looked down; gave a slight start; then his face became once more cold, apathetic.

"Who are you? What do you want?" he said roughly.

The countenance of the fellow who had ventured to accost the nobleman fell; a vindictive light shone from his eyes.

"It's like a drama at old Drury," he observed, with a slight sneer. "Only your lordship should have said: 'Who the devil are you?'"

Lord Ronsdale looked before him to where, in the distance, near a street lamp, the figure of a policeman might be dimly discerned; then, with obvious intention, he started toward the officer; but the man stepped in front of him. "No, you don't," he said.

The impassive, steel-like glance of Ronsdale played on the man; a white, shapely hand began to reach out. "One moment, and I'll give you in charge as--"

The fellow saw that Ronsdale meant it; he had but an instant to decide; a certain air of cheap, jaunty assurance he had begun to assume vanished. "All right," he said quickly, but with a ring of suppressed venom in his voice. "I'll be off. Your lordship has it all your own way since the Lord Nelson went down." There was a note of bitterness in his tones. "Besides, Dandy Joe's not exactly a favorite at headquarters just now, after the drubbing John Steele gave him."

"John Steele!" Lord Ronsdale looked abruptly round.

The fellow regarded him and ventured to go on: "I was witness for the police and Mr. Gillett, and he--Steele," with a curse, "had me on the stand. He knows every rook and welsher and every swell magsman, and all their haunts and habits. And he knows me--blame--" he made use of another expression more forcible--"if he don't know me as well as if he'd once been a pal. And now," in an injured tone, "Mr. Gillett calls me hard names for bringing discredit, as he terms it, on the force."

"What's this to me?"

The fellow stopped short in what he was saying; his small eyes glistened and he took a step forward. "Your lordship remembers the 'Frisco Pet? Your lordship remembers him?" he repeated, thrusting an alert face closer.

"I believe there was a prize-fighter of that name," was the calm reply.

"I say!" The fellow let his jaw fall slightly; he gazed at the nobleman with mingled shrewdness and admiration. "Your lordship remembers him only," with an accent, "as a patron of sport. Tossed a quid on him"--with a look of full meaning--"as your lordship would a bone to a dog. Perhaps," gaining in audacity, "your lordship would be so generous as to throw one or two now at one he once favored with his bounty."

"I--favored you? You lie!" The answer was concise; it cut like a lash; it robbed the man once more of all his hardihood. He slunk back.

"Very good," he muttered.

Lord Ronsdale turned and with a sharp swish of his cane walked on. The other, his eyes resentfully bright, looked after the tall, aristocratic, slowly departing figure.

As the nobleman ascended the steps of his club he seemed again to be thinking deeply; within, his preoccupation did not altogether desert him. In a corner, with the big pages of the Times before him, he read with scant interest the doings of the day; even a perennial telegram concerning a threatened invasion of England did not awaken momentary interest. He passed it over as casually as he did the markets, or a grudging, conservative item from the police courts, all that the blue pencil had left of the hopeful efforts of some poor penny-a-liner. From the daily fulminator he had turned to the weekly medium of fun and fooling, when, from behind another paper, the face of a gray-haired, good-natured appearing person, quite different off the bench, chanced to look out at him.

"Eh? That you, Ronsdale?" he said, reaching for a steaming glass of hot beverage at his elbow. "What do you think of it, this talk of an invasion by the Monseers?"

"Don't think anything of it."

"Answered in the true spirit of a Briton!" laughed the other. "I fancy, too, it'll be a long time before John Bull ceases to stamp around, master of his own shores, or Britannia no longer rules the deep. But how is your friend, Sir Charles Wray? I had the pleasure of meeting him the other morning in the court room."

"Same as usual, I imagine, Judge Beeson."

"And his fair niece, she takes kindly to the town and its gaieties?"

"Very kindly," dryly.

"A beautiful girl, our young Australian!" The elder man toyed with his glass, stirred the contents and sipped. "By the way, didn't I see John Steele in their box at the opera the other night?"

"It is possible," shortly.

"Rising man, that!" observed the other lightly. "Combination of brains and force! Did you ever notice his fist? It might belong to a prize-fighter, except that the hands are perfectly kept! You'd know at once he was a man accustomed to fighting, who would sweep aside obstacles, get what he wanted!"

"Think so?" Lord Ronsdale smoked steadily. "You, as a magistrate, I suppose, know him well?"

"Should hardly go that far; taciturn chap, don't you know! I don't believe any one really knows him."

"Or about him?" suggested the other, crossing his legs nonchalantly.

"Not much; only that he is an alien."

"An alien?" quickly. "Not a colonial?"

"No; he has lived in the colonies--Tasmania, and so on. But by birth he's an American."

"An American, eh? And practising at the British bar?"

"Not the first case of the kind; exceptions have been made before, and aliens 'called,' as we express it. Steele's hobby of criminology brought him to London, and his earnestness and ability in that line procured for him the privilege he sought. As member of the incorporated society that passes upon the qualifications of candidates it was my pleasure to sit in judgment on him; we raked him fore and aft but, bless you, he stood squarely on his feet and refused to be tripped."

"So he came to England to pursue a certain line?" said Lord Ronsdale half to himself.

"A man with a partiality for criminal work would naturally look to the modern Babylon. Steele apparently works more to gratify that predilection than for any reward in pounds and pence. Must have private means; have known him to spend a deal of time and money on cases there couldn't have been a sixpence in."

"How'd he happen to get down in Tasmania? Odd place for a Yankee!"

"That's one of the questions he wasn't asked," laughingly. "Perhaps what our Teutonic friends would call the Wander-lust took him there." Rising, "My compliments to Sir Charles when you see him."

Lord Ronsdale remained long at the club and the card-table that night; over the bits of pasteboard, however, his zest failed to flare high, although instinctively he played with a discernment that came from long practice. But the sight of a handful of gold pieces here, of a little pile there, the varying shiftings of the bright disks, as the vagaries of chance sent them this way or that, seemed to move him in no great degree,--perhaps because the winning or losing of a few hundred pounds, more or less, would have small effect on his fortunes or misfortunes. At a late, or rather, early, hour he pushed back his chair, richer by a few coins that jingled in his pocket, and, yawning, walked out. Summoning a cab, he got in, but as he found himself rattling homeward to the chambers he had taken in a fashionable part of town, he was aware that any emotions of annoyance and discontent experienced earlier that night, had suffered no abatement.

"Tasmania!" The horse's hoofs beat time to vague desultory thoughts; he stared out, perhaps, in fancy, at southern seas, looked up at stars more lustrous than those that hung over him now. Then the divers clusters of points, glowing, insistent, swam around, and he fell into a half doze, from which he was awakened by the abrupt stopping of the cab. Having paid the man he went up to his rooms. On the table in an inner apartment, his study, something bright, white, met his gaze: a note in Jocelyn Wray's handwriting! Quickly he reached for it and tore it open.

"A party of us ride in the park to-morrow morning. Will you join us?"

That was all; brief and to the point; Lord Ronsdale frowned.

"A party!" That would include John Steele perhaps. Once before on a morning, the girl's fair face and dancing eyes had wooed Steele away from his desk, or the court, to the park.

Should he go? The note slipped from his fingers to the carpet; he permitted it to lie there; the importance to himself and others of his decision he little realized. Could he have foreseen all that was involved by his going, or staying away, he would not so carelessly have thrown off his clothes and retired, dismissing the matter until the morrow, or rather, until he should chance to waken.

CHAPTER V

IN THE PARK

Close at hand, the trees in Hyde Park seemed to droop their branches, as if in sympathy with the gray aspect of the day, while afar, across the green, the sylvan guardians of the place had either receded altogether in the gray haze or stood forth like shadowy ghosts. In the foreground, not far from the main entrance, a number of sheep and their young nibbled contentedly the wet and delectable grass, and as some bright gown paused or whisked past, the juxtaposition of fine raiment and young lamb suggested soft, shifting Bouchers or other dainty French pastorals in paint. The air had a tang; the dampness enhanced the perfumes, made them fuller and sweeter, and a joyous sort of melancholy seemed to hold a springtime world in its grasp.

Into this scene of rural tranquillity rode briskly about the middle of the morning Jocelyn Wray and others. The glow on the girl's cheeks harmonized with the redness of her lips; the sparkling blue eyes mocked at all neutral hues; her gown and an odd ribbon or two waved, as it were, light defiance to motionless things--still leaves and branches, flowers and buds, drowsy and sleeping. Her mount was deep black, with fine arching neck and spirited head; on either side of the head, beneath ears sensitive, delicately pointed, had been fastened a rose, badge of favor from a bunch nestling at the white throat of the young girl. She rode with a grace and rhythmical ease suggestive of large experience in the pastime; the slender, supple figure swayed as if welcoming gladly the swing and the quick rush of air. Sometimes at her side, again just behind, galloped the horse bearing John Steele, and, as they went at a fair pace, preceded and followed by others of a gay party, the eyes of many passers-by turned to regard them.

"By Jove, they're stunning! It isn't often you see a man put up like that."

"Or a girl more the picture of health!"

"And beauty!"

Unconscious of these and other comments from the usual curious contingent of idlers filling the benches or strolling along the paths, the girl now set a yet swifter gait, glancing quickly over her shoulder at her companion: "Do you like a hard gallop? Shall we let them out?"

His brightening gaze answered; they touched their horses and for some distance raced madly on, passed those in front and left them far behind. Now Steele's eyes rested on the playing muscles of her superb horse, then lifted to the lithe form of Jocelyn Wray, the straight shoulders, a bit of a tress, disordered, floating rebelliously to the wind.

As abruptly as she had pressed her horse to that inspiring speed, she drew him in to a walk. "Wasn't that worth coming to the park for?" she said gaily.

He looked at her, at the flowers she readjusted, at the lips, half-parted to her quick breath.

"More than worth it."

"You see what you missed in the past," she observed in a tone slightly mocking.

"You were not here to suggest it," he returned quietly, with gaze only for blue eyes.

She suffered them to linger. "I suppose I should feel nattered that a suggestion from little me--"

"A suggestion from little you would, I fancy, go a long ways with many people." A spark shone now in the man's steady look; the girl seemed not afraid of it.

"I am fortunate," she laughed. "A compliment from Mr. John Steele!"

"Why not say--the truth?" he observed.

She stroked her horse's glossy neck and smiled furtively at the soft, velvet surface. "The truth?" she replied. "What is it? Where shall we find it? Isn't it something the old philosophers were always searching for? Plato, and--some of the others we were taught of in school."

He started as if to speak, but his answer remained unuttered; the man's lips closed tighter; a moment he watched the small gloved hand, then his gaze turned to the gray sky.

"So you see, I call compliments, compliments," she ended lightly.

He offered no comment; the horses moved on; suddenly she looked at him. One of those odd changes she had once or twice noticed before had come over John Steele; his face appeared too grave, too reserved; she might almost fancy a stormy play of emotion behind that mask of immobility. The girl's long lashes lowered; a slightly puzzled expression shone from her eyes. It may be she had but the natural curiosity of her sex, that her interest was compelled, because, although she had studied this man from various standpoints, his personality, strong, direct in some ways, she seemed unable to fathom. The golden head tilted; she allowed an impression of his profile to grow upon her.

"Do you know," she laughingly remarked, "you are not very interesting?"

He started. "Interesting!"

"A penny for your thoughts!" ironically.

"They're not worth it."

"No?"

He bent a little nearer; she swept back the disordered lock; an instant the man seemed to lose his self-possession. "Ah," he began, as if the words forced themselves from his lips, "if only I might--"

What he had been on the point of saying was never finished; the girl's quick glance, sweeping an instant ahead, had lingered on some one approaching from the opposite direction, and catching sight of him, she had just missed noting that swift alteration in John Steele's tones, the brief abandonment of studied control, a flare of irresistible feeling.

"Isn't that Lord Ronsdale?" asked the girl, continuing to gaze before her.

A black look replaced the sudden flame in Steele's gaze; the hand holding the reins closed on them tightly.

"Rather early for him, I fancy," she said, regarding the slim figure of the approaching rider. "With his devotion to clubs and late hours, you know! Do you, Mr. Steele, happen to belong to any of his clubs?"

"No." He spoke in a low voice, almost harshly.

Her brow lifted; his face was turned from her. Had he been mindful he might have noted a touch of displeasure on the proud face, that she regarded him as from a vague, indefinite distance.

"Lord Ronsdale is a very old friend of my uncle's," she observed severely, "and--mine!"

Was it that she had divined a deep-seated prejudice or hostility toward the nobleman hidden in John Steele's breast, that she took this occasion to let him know definitely that her friends were her friends? "Even when I was only a child he was very nice to me," she went on.

He remained silent; she frowned, then turned to the nobleman with a smile. Lord Ronsdale found that her greeting left nothing to be desired; she who had been somewhat unmindful of him lately on a sudden seemed really glad to see him. His slightly tired, aristocratic face lightened; the sunshine of Jocelyn Wray's eyes, the tonic of youth radiating from her, were sufficient to alleviate, if not dispel, ennui or lassitude.

"So good of you!" she murmured conventionally, as Steele dropped slightly back among the others who had by this time drawn near. "To arrive at such an unfashionable hour, I mean!"

His pleased but rather suspicious eyes studied her; he answered lightly; behind them now, he who had been riding with my lady could hear their gay laughter. Lord Ronsdale was apparently telling her a whimsical story; he had traveled much, met many people, bizarre and otherwise, and could be ironically witty when stimulated to the effort. John Steele did not look at them; when the girl at a turn in the way allowed her glance a moment to sweep aside toward those following, she could see he was riding with head slightly down bent.

"Good-looking beggar, isn't he," observed the nobleman suddenly, his gaze sharpened on her.

"Who?" asked the girl.

"That chap, Steele," he answered insinuatingly.

"Is he?" Her voice was flute-like. "What is that noise?" abruptly.

"Noise?" Lord Ronsdale listened. "That's music, or supposed to be! Unless I am mistaken, The Campbells are Coming," he drawled.

"The Campbells? Oh, I understand! Let us wait!"

They drew in their horses; the black one became restive, eyed with obvious disapproval a gaily bedecked body of men swinging smartly along toward them. At their head marched pipers, blowing lustily; behind strode doughty clansmen, heads up, as became those carrying memories of battles won. They approached after the manner of veterans who felt that they deserved tributes of admiration from beholders: that in the piping times of peace they were bound to be conquerors still.

Louder shrieked the wild concords; bare legs flashed nearer; bright colors flaunted with startling distinctness. And at the sight and sound, the girl's horse, unaccustomed to the pomp and pride of martial display, began to plunge and rear. She spoke sharply; tried to control it but found she could not. Lord Ronsdale saw her predicament but was powerless to lend assistance, being at the moment engaged in a vigorous effort to prevent his own horse from bolting.

The bagpipes came directly opposite; the black horse reared viciously; for the moment it seemed that Jocelyn would either be thrown or that the affrighted animal would fall over on her, when a man sprang forward and a hand reached up. He stood almost beneath the horse; as it came down a hoof struck his shoulder a glancing blow, grazed hard his arm, tearing the cloth. But before the animal could continue his rebellious tactics a hand like iron had reached for, grasped the bridle; those who watched could realize a great strength in the restraining fingers, the unusual power of Steele's muscles. The black horse, trembling, soon stood still; the bagpipes passed on, and Steele looked up at the girl.

"If you care to dismount--"

"Thank you," she said. "I'm not afraid. Especially," she added lightly, "with you at the bridle!"

"Few riders could have kept their seats so well," he answered, with ill-concealed admiration.

"I have always been accustomed to horses. In Australia we ride a great deal."

"For the instant," his face slightly paler, "I thought something would happen."

"It might have," she returned, a light in her eyes, "but for a timely hand. My horse apparently does not appreciate Scotch airs."

"Ugly brute!" Lord Ronsdale, a dissatisfied expression on his handsome countenance, approached. "A little of the whip--" the words were arrested; the nobleman stared at John Steele, or rather at the bare arm which the torn sleeve revealed well above the elbow.

The white, uplifted arm suddenly dropped; Steele drew the cloth quickly about it, but not before his eyes had met those of Lord Ronsdale and caught the amazement, incredulity, sudden terror--was it terror?--in their depths.

"Told you not to trust him, Jocelyn!" Sir Charles' loud, hearty voice at the same moment interrupted. "There was a look about him I didn't like from the beginning."

"Perhaps he needs only a little toning down to be fit," put in Captain Forsythe, as he and the others drew near. "A few seasons with the hounds, or--"

"Chasing some poor little fox!" said the girl with light scorn.

"One might be doing something worse!"

"One might!" Her accents were dubious.

"You don't believe in the chase, or the hunt? Allow me to differ; people always must hunt something, don't you know; primeval instinct! Used to hunt one another," he laughed. "Sometimes do now. Fox is only a substitute for the joys of the man-hunt; sort of sop to Cerberus, as it were. Eh, Ronsdale?"

But the nobleman did not answer; his face looked drawn and gray; with one hand he seemed almost clinging to his saddle. John Steele's back was turned; he was bending over the girth of his saddle and his features could not be seen, but the hand, so firm and assured a moment before, seemed a little uncertain as it made pretext to readjust a fastening or buckle.

"Why, man, you look ill!" Captain Forsythe, turning to Lord Ronsdale, exclaimed suddenly.

"It's--nothing--much--" With vacant expression the nobleman regarded the speaker; then lifted his hand and pressed it an instant to his breast. "Heart," he murmured mechanically. "Beastly bad heart, you know, and sometimes a little thing--slight shock--Miss Wray's danger--"

"Take some of this!" The captain, with solicitude, pressed a flask on him; the nobleman drank deeply. "There; that'll pick you up."

"Beastly foolish!" A color sprang to Lord Ronsdale's face; he held himself more erect.

"Not at all!" Sir Charles interposed. "A man can't help a bad liver or a bad heart. One of those inscrutable visitations of Providence! But shall we go on? You're sure you're quite yourself?"

"Quite!" The nobleman's tone was even harder and more metallic than usual; his thin lips compressed to a tight line; his eyes that looked out to a great distance were bright and glistening.

"Are you ready, Mr. Steele?" Jocelyn Wray waited a moment as the others started, looked down at that gentleman. Her voice was gracious; its soft accents seemed to say: "You may ride with me; it is your reward!"

For one restored so quickly to favor, with a felicitous prospect of gay words and bright glances, John Steele seemed singularly dull and apathetic. He exhibited no haste in the task he was engaged in; straightened slowly and mounted with leisure. Once again in the saddle, and on their way, it is true he appeared to listen to the girl; but his responses were vague, lacking both in vivacity and humor. It was impossible she should not notice this want of attention; she bit her lips once; then she laughed.

"Do you know, Mr. Steele, if I were vain I should feel hurt."

"Hurt?" he repeated.

"You haven't heard what I have been saying." Her eyes challenged his.

"Haven't I?"

"Deny it."

He did not; again she looked at him merrily.

"Of course, I can't afford to be harsh with my rescuer. Perhaps"--in the same tone--"you really did save my life! Have you ever really saved any one--any one else, shall I say?--you who are so strong?"

A spasm as of pain passed over his face; his look, however, was not for her; and the girl's eyes, too, had now become suddenly set afar. Was she thinking of another scene, some one her own words conjured to mind? Her mood seemed to gain in seriousness; she also became very quiet; and so almost in silence they went on to the entrance, down the street, to her home.

"Au revoir, and thank you!" she said there, regaining her accustomed lightness.

"Good-by! At least for the present," he added. "I am leaving London," abruptly.

"Leaving?" She regarded him in surprise. "To be gone long?"

"It is difficult to say. Perhaps."

"But--you must have decided suddenly?"

"Yes."

"While we have been riding home?" Again he answered affirmatively; the blue eyes looked at him long. "Is it--is it serious?"

"A little."

"Men make so much of business, nowadays," she observed, "it--it always seems serious, I suppose. We--we are moving into the country in a few weeks. Shall I--shall we, see you before then?"

"To my regret, I am afraid not."

"And after"--in a voice matter-of-fact--"I think aunt has put you down for July; a house party; I don't recall the exact dates. You will come?"

"Shall we say, circumstances permitting--" "Certainly," a little stiffly, "circumstances permitting." She gave him her hand. "Au revoir! Or good-by, if you prefer it." He held the little gloved fingers; let them drop. There was a suggestion of hopelessness in the movement that fitted oddly his inherent vigor and self-poise; she started to draw away; an ineffable something held her.

"Good luck in your business!" she found herself saying, half-gaily, half-ironically.

He answered, hoarsely, something--what?--rode off. With color flaming high, the girl looked after him until Lord Ronsdale's horse, clattering near, caused her to turn quickly.

CHAPTER VI

A CONFERENCE

The book-worms' row, hardly a street, more a short-cut passage between two important thoroughfares, had through the course of many years exercised a subtle fascination for pedant, pedagogue or itinerant litterateur. At one end of the way was rush and bustle; at the other, more rush and bustle; here might be found the comparative hush of the tiny stream that for a short interval has left the parent current. Dusty and musty shops looked out on either side, and within on shelves, or without on stands, unexpected bargains lay carelessly about, rare Horaces or Ovids, Greek tragedies, ponderous volumes of the golden age of the English poets and philosophers. Truth nestled in dark corners; knowledge lay hidden in frayed covers and beauty enshrined herself behind cobwebs.

Not that the thoroughfare, in its entirety, was devoted to books; nor that it housed no other people than bibliomaniacs or antiquarians! Higher, above the little shops, small rooms, reached by rickety stairways, offered quiet corners for divers and sundry gentlemen whose occupations called for discreet and retired nooks.

In one of these places, described on the door as "a private, confidential, inquiry office," sat, on the morning following John Steele's ride in the park, a little man with ferret-like eyes at a dusty desk near a dusty window. He did not seem to be very busy, was engaged at the moment in drawing meaningless cabalistic signs on a piece of paper, when a step in the hallway and a low tapping at the door caused him to throw down his pen and straighten expectantly. A client, perhaps!--a woman?--no, a man! With momentary surprise, he gazed on the delicately chiseled features of his caller; a gentleman faultlessly dressed and wearing a spring flower in his coat.

"Mr. Gillett?" The visitor's glance veiled an expression of restlessness; his face, although mask-like, was tinted with a faint flush.

The police agent at once rose. "The same, sir, at your service; I--but I beg your pardon; unless I am mistaken--haven't we--"

"Yes; a number of years ago on the Lord Nelson," said the caller in a hard matter-of-fact tone. "We were fellow passengers on her, until--"

"We became fellow occupants of one of her small boats! An aging experience! But won't you," with that deference for rank and position those of his type are pleased to assume, "honor me by being seated, Lord Ronsdale?"

As he spoke, he dusted vigorously with his handkerchief a chair which his caller, after a moment's hesitation, sank into; Mr. Gillett regarded the one he himself had been occupying; then, in an apologetic manner ventured to take it. "Your lordship is well? Your lordship looks it. Your lordship was, last I heard, in Australia, I believe. A genuine pleasure to see your lordship once more."

The visitor offered no acknowledgment to this flattering effusion; his long fingers rubbed one another softly. He looked at the table, the window, anywhere save at the proprietor of the establishment, then said: "I saw by an advertisement in the morning papers that you had severed your connection with the force and had opened this--a private consultation bureau."

"Quite so!" The other looked momentarily embarrassed. "A little friction--account of some case--unreliable witness that got tangled up--They undertook to criticize me, after all my faithful service--" He broke off. "Besides, the time comes when a man realizes he can do better for himself by himself. I am now devoting myself to a small, but strictly high-class," with an accent, "clientele."

Lord Ronsdale considered; when he spoke, his voice was low, but it did not caress the ear. "You know John Steele, of course?"

The ferret eyes snapped. "That I do, your Lordship. What of him?" quickly.

The caller made no reply but tapped the floor lightly with his cane, and--"What of him?" repeated Mr. Gillett.

Lord Ronsdale's glance turned; it had a strange brightness. His next question was irrelevant. "Ever think much about the Lord Nelson, Gillett?"

"She isn't a boat one's apt to forget, after what happened, your Lordship," was the answer. "And if I do say it, her passengers were of the kind to leave pleasant recollections," the police agent diplomatically added.

"Her passengers?" The caller's thin lips compressed; a spark seemed to leap from his gaze, but not before he had dropped it. "Among them, if memory serves me, were a number of convicts?"

"A job lot of precious jailbirds that I was acting as escort of, your Lordship!"

"But who never reached Australia!" quickly.

"Drowned!--every mother's son of them!" observed Mr. Gillett, with a possible trace of complacency. "Not that I fancy the country they were going to mourned much about that. I understand a strong sentiment's growing out there against that sort of immigration."

The visitor's white hand held closer the head of his cane; the stick bent to his weight. "Were they all drowned, by the way?" he observed as if seeking casual information on some subject that had partly passed from his mind.

"No doubt of it. They were not released until the second boat got off, and then there was no time to get overboard the life rafts!"

"True." Lord Ronsdale gazed absently out of the window, through a film, as it were, at a venerable figure below; one of the species helluo librorum standing before a book-stall opposite. "Recall the day on that memorable voyage you were telling us about them--who they were, and so on?"

"Very well," replied Mr. Gillett, good-humoredly. If his caller cared to discuss generalities rather than come at once to the business at hand, whatever had brought him there, that was none of his concern. These titled gentry had a leisurely method, peculiar to themselves, of broaching a subject; but if they paid him well for his time he could afford to appear an amiable and interested listener. In this case, the thought also insinuated itself, that his visitor had something of the manner of a man who had been up late the night before; the glint of his eye was that of your fashionable gamester; Mr. Gillett smiled sympathetically.

"One, if I recall rightly," went on Lord Ronsdale, "was known as--let me see"--the elastic stick described a sharper curve--"the 'Frisco Pet? Remember?" He bent slightly nearer.

"That I do. Not likely to forget him. Unmanageable; one of the worst! Was transported for life, with death as a penalty for returning." A slight sound came from the nobleman's throat. "A needless precaution," laughed the speaker, "for he's gone to his reward. And so your lordship remembers--"

"I remember when he used to step into the ring," said Lord Ronsdale, his voice rising somewhat. "Truth is, sight of you brought back old recollections. Things I haven't thought of for a long time, don't you see!"

"Quite so! Delighted, I am sure. I didn't know so much about him then; that came after; except that the gentlemen found him a figure worth looking at when he got up at the post--"

"Yes; he was worth looking at." Lord Bonsdale's eyes half closed. "A heavy-fisted, shapely brute; with muscles like steel. But ignorant--" He lingered on the word; then his glance suddenly lifted--"Had something on his arm; recall noticing it while the bout was on!"

Mr. Gillett with a knowing expression rose, took a volume from a bookcase and opened it.

"The 'something' you speak of, my Lord," he observed proudly, "should be here; I will show it that you may appreciate my system; the method I have of gathering and tabulating data. You will find an encyclopedia of information in that bookcase. All that Scotland Yard has, and perhaps a little besides."

"Really?" The nobleman's eyes fastened themselves on the book.

"To illustrate: Here's his case." Gillett's fingers moved lightly over the page. "'Testimony of Dandy Joe, down-stairs at the time with landlady who kept the house where the crime was committed. Heard 'Frisco Pet, who had been drinking, come in; go up-stairs, as they supposed, to his own room; shortly after, loud voices; pistol shot. Landlady and Joe found woman, Amy Gerard, dead in shabby little sitting-room. Pet, the worse for liquor, in a dazed condition at a table, head in his hands. Testimony of Joe corroborated by landlady; she swore no one had been in house except parties here mentioned, all lodgers.

"'Private mem.--House in bad neighborhood, near the Adelphi catacombs. Son of landlady, red-headed giant, also one-time prize-fighter, used to live here; the Pet's last fight in the ring was with him. Later Tom took to the road; was wanted by the police at the time of the crime for some brutal highway work--' But," breaking off, "I am wearying your lordship. Here is what I was especially looking for, the markings on the arm of the 'Frisco Pet. Perhaps, however, your lordship doesn't care to listen further--"

"Go on!" The words broke sharply from the visitor's lips; then he gave a metallic laugh. "I am interested in this wonderful system of yours."

Mr. Gillett read slowly: "'On the right arm of the 'Frisco Pet, just below the elbow, appears the figure of a man, in sparring attitude, done in sailor's tattooing; about the waist a flag, the stars and stripes in their accustomed colors; crudely drawn but not to be mistaken by noting following defects and details--' which," closing the book, "I won't read."

IIis lordship's head had turned; at first he did not speak. "A good system," he remarked after an interval. "And a very good description, and yet--" His voice died away; for a moment he sat motionless. "But my purpose--the purpose of my visit--I--we have wandered quite from that. Let us, I beg of you, talk business."

Mr. Gillett started as if to venture a mild expostulation, but thought better of the impulse. "What is your lordship's business with me?" he observed in his most professional tone.

"I believe"--the visitor moistened his lips--"I believe I mentioned--John Steele when I came in?"

"Your lordship did."

"It--concerns him."

"I am all attention, your Lordship." Mr. Gillett's manner was keen, energetic; if he felt surprise he suppressed it. "Good! your lordship's business concerns John Steele."

"For reasons that need not be mentioned, I want to find out all I can about him. That, I believe, is the sort of work you undertake. The terms for your services can be arranged later. It is unnecessary to say you will be well paid. I assume you can command competent and trustworthy help, that you have agents, perhaps, in other countries?"

Mr. Gillett nodded. "If your lordship would give me some idea of the scope of the inquiry--"

The long fingers opened, then closed tightly.

"In the first place, you are to ascertain where John Steele was before he came to England; how he got there; what he did. Naturally, if he has lived in a far-away port you would seek to know the ship that brought him there; the names of the captain and the crew."

"Your lordship thinks, then, our investigation may lead us to distant lands?"

"Who can tell?" The nobleman's voice was sharp, querulous. "That is what you are to find out."

"It shall be done, your Lordship," replied the other quickly. "I shall embark in the matter with great zest, and, I may add, interest."

"Interest?" The nobleman looked at him. "Oh, yes!"

"If I might be so bold, may I ask, does your lordship expect to find anything that would--ahem!--cast any reflection on the high standing John Steele is building up for himself in the community, or---"

A shadow seemed to darken the mask-like features of the visitor; his gaze at once glittering, vaguely questioning, was fastened on the wall; then slowly, without answering, he got up. "Surmises are not to enter into this matter," he said shortly. "It is facts, I want--facts!"

"And your lordship shall have them. The case appears simple; not hard to get at the bottom of!" An odd expression shone from the visitor's eyes. "Which reminds me he has left town," added Gillett.

"Left town!" Lord Ronsdale wheeled abruptly. "You mean--"

"For a little trip to the continent I should imagine; heard of it because he got some unimportant court matter put over."

"Gone away!" The nobleman, his back to the other, lifted a hand to his brow. "When?"

"Last night."

"It was only yesterday morning I was riding with him!"

"And he didn't mention the matter?"

The visitor did not answer. "Why should he have gone away?" he murmured, half aloud. "Was it because--" He walked to the door; at the threshold stopped and looked back. "You might begin your inquiry by learning all you can about this little trip," he suggested. "And by the by, whatever you may find out, if anything, you will regard as belonging to me exclusively; to be mentioned, under no circumstances, without my permission, to any one whosoever--"

"Your lordship!" Mr. Gillett's hurt voice implied the little need for such admonition. "In my profession absolute integrity toward one's client demands that secrecy should be the first con--"

"It is understood then. Let me hear from you from time to time," and the nobleman went out.

Mr. Gillett looked after him, then, reflectively, at the closed door. Outside the sound of shuffling feet alone broke the stillness; before the book-stand the bibliomaniac buried his face deeper in the musty pages of an old tragedy.

CHAPTER VII

Several months went by and John Steele saw nothing further, although he heard often, of Miss Jocelyn Wray. His business to the continent, whatever its nature, had seemed sufficiently important to authorize from him to her, in due process of time, a short perfunctory message regretting his inability to present himself at the appointed hour at Strathorn House. Whether the young girl found in the letter a vagueness warranting a suspicion that John Steele preferred the heavy duties of the city to the light frivolities of the country matters not; suffice it the weeks passed and no further invitations, in the ponderous script of the wife of Sir Charles, arrived to tempt him from his accustomed ways. But the days of this long interim had not passed altogether uneventfully; a few incidents, apart from the routine of his work, obtruded themselves upon his attention.

A number of supposedly prospective clients had called to ask for him at his office during his sojourn on the other side of the channel. That was to have been expected; but one or two of these, by dint of flattery, or possibly silver-lined persuasion, had succeeded in gaining access to his chambers.

"I should like to have a look into John Steele's library; I've heard it's worth while," one had observed to the butler at the door. "Only a bit of a peep around!" His manner of putting his desire, supplemented by a half-crown, left the butler no alternative save to comply with the request, until the "peep around" began to develop into more than cursory examination, when his sense of propriety became outraged and the visitor's welcome was cut short.

"He was that curious, a regular Paul Pry!" explained the servant to John Steele, in narrating the incident on the latter's return to London. "Seemed specially taken by the reports of the old trials you have on the shelves, sir. 'What an interesting collection of causes célèbres!' he kept remarking. 'I suppose your master makes much of them?' He would have been handling of them, too, and when I showed him the door--trusting I did right, sir, even if he should happen to be a client!--he asked more questions before going."

"What questions?" quietly.

"Personal-like. But I put a stop to that."

For a few moments John Steele said nothing; his face, on his reappearance in London, had looked slightly paler, more set and determined, not unlike that of a man, who, strongly assailed, has made up his mind to do battle to the end. With whom? How many? He might put out his hand, clench it; the thin air made no answer. He regarded the shadows now; they seemed to wave around him, intangible, obscure. A dark day in town, the streets were oppressive; the people below passed like poorly done replicas of themselves; the rattle of the wheels resembled a sullen, disgruntled mumble.

"You will admit no one to my chambers during my absence in the future," said Steele at length, to the man, sternly. "No one, you understand, under any pretext whatever; even," a flicker of grim humor in the deep eyes, "if he should say he was a client of mine!"

The butler returned a subdued answer, and John Steele, after a moment's thought, stepped to a large safe in the corner, and applying a somewhat elaborate combination, swung open the door. Taking from a compartment a bundle of papers carefully rolled, he unfastened the tape, spread them on a table and examined them, one after the other. They made a voluminous heap; here and there on the white pages in bold regular script appeared the name of a woman; her life lay before him, the various stages of an odd and erratic career. At a cabaret at Montmartre; at a casino in the Paris Bohemian quarter; in London--at a variety hall of amusement. And afterward!--wastrel, nomad! Throughout the writing, in many of the documents, another name, too, a titled name, a man's, often came and went, flitted elusively from leaf to leaf.

Illustration: Here and there appeared the name of a woman

Here and there appeared the name of a woman Page

The reader looked at this name, wrote a page or two, and inserted them. But his task seemed to afford him little satisfaction; his face wore an expression not remote from discouragement; none knew better than he the actual value, for his purpose, of the material before him. The chaff, froth, bubble of the case!--almost contemptuously he regarded it. Had he sought the unattainable? Certainly he had left no stone unturned, no stone, and yet the head and front of what he sought had ever escaped him--should he ever grasp it?--with these new secret activities menacing him?--harassing the future?

He drew himself up suddenly, as if to shake off momentary doubt or depression. Replacing his documents in the safe and locking it, he walked into a room adjoining; in a bare, square place on the wall hung foils and broadswords, and the only furnishings were the conventional appointments of a home gymnasium.

Here, having doffed his street clothes and assumed the scant costume of the athlete, for an hour or more he exercised vigorously, every muscle responding to its task with an untiring ease that told of a perfect system of training. As he stood in the glow, breathing deep and full, his figure, with its perfect lines of strength and litheness, the superb but not too pronounced swell of limb and shoulder, would have been the delight of the professional expounder of dumb-bells, bars and clubs, as the most proper medium of "fitness" and condition. Whether he exercised for the sake of exercising, or because bodily movement served to stimulate his mind in the consideration of problems of moment, John Steele certainly had never been in finer physical fettle than at this particular period of his varied and eventful career. Which proved of service to him and his well-being, for one night, not long thereafter, he was called upon to defend himself from a number of footpads who set upon him.

The episode occurred in his own street near a corner, where the shadows were black at an hour when the narrow way seemed silent and deserted. For a block or more footfalls had sounded behind him, now quickening, then becoming more deliberate, in unison with his own steps, as from time to time he purposely altered his pace. Once he had stopped; whereupon they too had paused. A moment he stood looking up at St. Paul's, immense, ominous, casting at that late hour a dim patch of shadow over scores of pigmy buildings and paltry byways; when he went on, patter!--patter!--the trailing of feet, inevitable as fate, followed through the darkness. But they came no nearer until, abruptly wheeling, he entered the short street where his chambers were located; at the same time two men, apparently sauntering from the river in that side thoroughfare, approached him somewhat rapidly, separating slightly as they did so.

John Steele seemed oblivious. He moved into a doorway and drawing from his pocket a cigar, unconcernedly lighted a match. The fellows looked at him, at the tiny flame; it flickered and went out. They hesitated; he felt in his pocket, giving them time to move by. They did not do so; in a moment the others from the main highway would join them. As if disappointed in not finding what he sought, Steele, looking around, appeared to see for the first time the evil-looking miscreants who had came from the direction of the Thames, and striding toward them asked bruskly for a light. One of the fellows thus unceremoniously addressed had actually begun to feel in his shabby garments for the article required when his companion uttered a short derisory oath.

It served as a sudden stimulus to him against whom it was directed; the old precept that he who strikes first strikes best, John Steele seemed fully to appreciate. His heavy stick flashed in the air, rang hard; the way before him cleared, he did not linger. But close behind now the others came fast; his door, however, was near. Now he reached it, fitted the heavy key. Had it turned as usual, the episode would have been brought to a speedy conclusion, but, as it was, the key stuck. The foremost of those who had been trailing fell upon Steele but soon drew back; one of them, unable to repress a groan, held his hand to a broken wrist, while from his helpless fingers a knife dropped to the ground.

A hoarse voice in thieves' jargon, unintelligible to the layman, cursed them for cowards; John Steele on a sudden laughed loudly, exultantly; whereupon he who had thus spoken from the background stared. A ponderous, hulking fellow, about six feet three, with a shock of red hair and a thick hanging lip,--obviously this one of his assailants possessed immense, unusual strength. In appearance he was the reverse of pleasing; his bloodshot eyes seemed to shine like coals from the darkness, the huge body to quiver with rage or with lust for the conflict.

"Let me at him, ye--!" he cried in foul and flash tongue, when John Steele suddenly called him by name, said something in that selfsame dialect of pickpurses and their ilk.

Whatever the words or their portent, the effect was startling. Steele's bulky assailant paused, remained stock-still, his purpose arrested, all his anger gone out of him.

"How the--? Who--?" the man began.

"Call off your fellows!" John Steele's voice seemed to thrill; a fierce elation shone from his glance. "I want to talk with you. It'll be more worth your while than any prigging or bagging you've ever yet done."

"Well, I'm blowed!" The man's tone was puzzled; surprise, suspicion gleamed from the bloodshot eyes. "How should a swell gent like you know--? And you want to talk with me? Here's a gamey cove!"

"I tell you I must talk with you! And it will be better for you, my man--" a sharp metallic click told that the speaker had turned the key in the lock behind him--"to step in here with me. You needn't be afraid I'm going to nab you; I've got a lay better than hooking you for the dock. As for the others, they can go, for all of me."

"Oh, they can!" The big man's face expressed varying feelings--vague wonder; at the same time he began to edge cautiously away. "That would be a nice plant, wouldn't it? Let's out of this, blokies!" suddenly, "this cove knows too much, and--"

"Wait!" Steele stepped slightly toward him. "I want you, Tom Rogers, and I'm going to have you; it'll be quids in your pocket and not Newgate."

"Slope for it, mates!" The big man's voice rang out; around the corner in the direction of the Thames the burly figure of a policeman appeared in the dim light. "That's his little game!" and turned.

But John Steele sprang savagely forward. "You fool! You'll not get away so easily!" he exclaimed, when one of the others put out a foot. It caught the pursuing man fairly and tripped him. John Steele went down hard; his head struck the stone curb violently.

For some moments he lay still; when at length he did move, to lift himself on his elbow, as through a mist he made out the broad and solicitous face of a policeman bending over him.

"That was a nasty fall you got, sir."

"Fall?" John Steele arose, stood swaying. "That man!--must not escape--Do you hear? must not!" As he spoke he made as if to rush forward; the other laid steadying fingers on his arm.

"Hold hard a bit, sir," he said. "Not quite yourself; besides, they're well out of sight now. No use running after."

Steele moved, grasped the railing leading up the front step; his brow throbbed; a thousand darting pains shot through his brain. But for the moment these physical pangs were as nothing; disappointment, self-reproach moved him. To have allowed himself to go down like that; to have been caught by such a simple trick! Clumsy clod!--and at a moment when-- He laughed fiercely; from his head the blood flowed; he did not feel that hurt now.

The officer regarded the strong, noble figure moving just a little to and fro, the lips set ironically, the dark eyes that gleamed in the night as with sardonic derision.

"Pardon me, sir," he said in a brisker tone, "but hadn't we better go in? This, I take it, is your house; you can look after yourself somewhat, and afterward describe your assailants. Then we'll start out to find and arrest them, if possible!"

"Arrest?" John Steele looked at the officer; his gaze slowly regained its accustomed steadiness. "I am afraid I can't help you; the darkness, the suddenness of the attack--"

"But surely you must have noticed something, sir; whether they were large, or small; what sort of clothes they wore--" The other shook his head; the man appeared disappointed. "Well, I'll make a report of the attack, but--"

Steele loosened his hold on the railing; he appeared now to have recovered his strength. "That's just what I don't want you to do. My name is John Steele, you know of me?" And, as the other returned a respectful affirmative, "It is my desire to escape any notoriety in this little matter, you understand? As one whose profession brings him in connection with these people, the episode seems rather anomalous as well as humiliating. It might even," his accents had a covert mocking sound, "furnish a paragraph for one of the comic weeklies. So you see--" Something passed from his hand to the policeman's.

"I didn't think of that, sir; but I suppose there is something in your way of looking at it, and as there isn't much chance of getting them, anyhow, without any clue, or description--" his voice died away.

Walking quickly up the steps John Steele opened the door, murmured a perfunctory "Good night" and let himself in. But as he mounted to his chambers, some of the moment's exultation that had seized him at sight of the man, revived.

"He has come back--he is here--in London. I surely can lay hands on him--I must! I will!"

CHAPTER VIII

A CHANGE OF FRONT

HE found the task no easy one, however, although he went at it with his characteristic vigor and energy. Few men knew the seamy side of London better than John Steele: its darksome streets and foul alleys, its hovels and various habitations. And this knowledge he utilized to the best advantage, always to find that his efforts came to naught. The snares he set before possible hiding-places proved abortive; the artifices he employed to uncover the quarry in maze or labyrinth were fruitless. The man had appeared like a vision from the past, and vanished. Whither? Out of the country, once more? Over the seas? Had he taken quick alarm at Steele's words, and effected a hasty retreat from the scenes of his graceless and nefarious career?

Reluctantly John Steele found himself forced to entertain the possibility of this being so; otherwise the facilities at his command were such that he should most likely, ere this, have been able to attain his end, find what he sought. Soberly attired, he attracted no very marked attention in the slums,--breeding spots of the criminal classes; the denizens knew John Steele; he had been there oft before.

He had, on occasion, assisted some of them with stern good advice or more substantial services. He was acquainted with these men and women; had, perhaps, a larger charity for them than most people find it expedient to cherish. His glance had always seemed to read them through and through, with uncompromising realization of their infirmities, weaknesses of the flesh and inherited moral imperfections. His very fearlessness had ever commended him to that lower world; it did now, enabling him the better to cast about in divers directions.

To hear nothing, to learn nothing, at least, very little! One man had seen the object of Steele's solicitude and to this person, a weazened little "undesirable," the red-headed giant had confided that London was pretty hot and he thought of decamping from it.

"'Arter all this time that's gone by,' he says to me, bitter-like, 'to think a man can't come back to 'is native 'ome without being spied on for what ought long ago to be dead and forgot!' But you're not trying to lay hands on 'im, to put 'im in the pen, gov'ner?"

"I?" A singular glint shot from Steele's gaze. "No, no, my man, I'm not seeking him for that. But he didn't say where he expected to go?"

"Not he."

"Nor what had brought him to London?"

"I expect it was 'omesickness, sir. 'E's been a bad lot, but 'e has a heart, arter all. It was to see 'is mother 'e came back; the old woman drew 'im 'ere. You see 'e had written 'er from foreign parts, but could never 'ear; 'cause she had moved; used to keep a place where a woman was found--"

"Dead?"

"Murdered!" said the man; John Steele was silent. "And she, 'is mother 'ad gone, 'aving saved a bit, out into a peaceable-like little 'amlet, where there weren't no bobbies, only instead, bits of flower gardens and bright bloomin' daffy-down-dillies. But, blime me, when Tom come and found out where she 'ad changed to, if she 'adn't gone and shuffled off, and all 'e 'ad for 'is pains was the sight of a mound in the churchyard."

"Yes; she's buried," said John Steele thoughtfully, "and all she might have told about the woman who was--murdered, is buried with her."

"But she did tell, sir; at the time," quickly, "of the trial."

"True." The visitor's tone changed. "If you can find Tom, give him this note; you'll be well paid--"

"I ain't askin' for that; you got me off easy once and gave me a lift, arter I was let out--"

"Well, well!" Steele made a brusk gesture. "We all need a helping hand sometimes," he said turning away.

And that was as near as he had come to attainment of his desires.

Summer passed; sometimes, the better to think, to plan, to keep himself girded by constant exercise, he repaired to the park, now neglected by fashion and given over to that nebulous quantity of diverse qualities called the people. Where fine gentlemen and beaux had idled, middle-class nurse-maids now trundled their charges or paused to converse with the stately guardians of the place. Almost deserted were roads and row; landau, victoria and brougham, with their varied coats-of-arms, no longer rolled pompously past; only the occasional democratic cab, of nimble possibilities, speeding by with a fare lent pretext of life to the scene. True, the nomad appeared in ever increasing numbers, holding his right to the sward for a couch as an inalienable privilege; John Steele encountered him on every hand. Once, beneath a great tree, where Jocelyn Wray and he had stopped their horses to talk for a moment, the bleared, bloated face of what had been a man looked up at him. The sight for an instant seemed to startle the beholder; a wave of anger at that face, set in a place where imagination had an instant before played with a picture altogether different, passed over him; then quickly went.

As he strode forward at a swinging pace, his thoughts swept swiftly again into another channel, one they had been flowing in when he had first entered the park that day. Above him the leaves rustled ceaselessly; their restless movements seemed in keeping with his mood wherein impatience mingled with other and fiercer emotions. Fate had been against him, the inevitable "what must be," which, in the end, crushes alike Faintheart or Strongheart. Of what avail to square his shoulders? the danger pressed close; he felt it, by that intuition men sometimes have. What if he left, left the field, this England? Who could accuse him of cowardice if in that black moment he yielded to the hateful course and went, like the guilty, pitiable skulkers?

"How do you do, Steele? Just the man I wanted to see!"

Near the main exit, toward which John Steele had unconsciously stepped, the sound of a familiar voice and the appearance of a well-known stocky form broke in, with startling abruptness, on the dark train of thought.

"Deep in some point of law?" went on Sir Charles. "'Pon honor, believe you would have cut me. However, don't apologize; you're forgiven!"

"Most amiable of you to say so, Sir Charles!" perfunctorily.

"Not at all! Especially as our meeting is quite apropos. Obliged to run up to town on a little matter of business; but, thank goodness, it's done. Never saw London more deserted. Dined at the club, nobody there. Supped at the hotel, dining-room empty. Strolled up Piccadilly, not a soul to be seen. That is," he added, "no one whom one has seen before, which is the same thing. But how did you enjoy your trip to the continent?"

"It was not exactly a trip for pleasure," returned the other with a slight accent of constraint.

"Ah, yes; so I understood. But fancy going to the continent on business! One usually goes for--which reminds me, how would you like to go back into the country with me?"

"I? It is impossible at the moment for--"

But Sir Charles seemed not to listen. "Deuced dull journey for a man to take alone; good deal of it by coach. You'll find a few salmon to kill--trout and all that. Think of the joy of whipping a stream, after having been mewed up all these months in the musty metropolis! Besides, I made a wager with Jocelyn you wouldn't refuse a second opportunity to bask in Arcadia." He laughed. "'I really couldn't presume to ask him again,' is the way she expressed it, 'but if you can draw a sufficiently eloquent picture of the rural attractions of Strathorn to woo him from his beloved dusty byways, you have my permission to try.'"

"Did she say that?" John Steele spoke quickly. Then, "I am sorry, it is impossible, but," in a low tone, "how is Miss Wray?"

"Never better. Enjoying every moment. Jolly party and all that. Lord Ronsdale and--" Here Sir Charles enumerated a number of people.

"Lord Ronsdale is there?"

"Yes; couldn't keep him away from Strathorn House now," he laughed. "As a matter of fact he has asked my permission to--there!" Sir Charles stopped, then laughed again with a little embarrassment. "I've nearly let the cat out of the bag."

John Steele spoke no word; his face was set, immovable; his lashes shaded his eyes. A flood of traffic at a corner held them; he appeared attentive only for it. The wheels pounded and rattled; the whips snapped and cracked.

"You mean he has proposed for her hand and she--" Steele seemed to speak with difficulty--"has consented?"

The noise almost drowned the question but Sir Charles heard.

"Well, not exactly. She appears complaisant, as it were," he answered. "But really, I shouldn't have mentioned the matter at all; quite premature, you understand. Let's say no more about it. And--what was it you said about going back with me?"

"Yes," said John Steele with a sudden strength and energy that Sir Charles might attribute to the desire to make himself understood above the din of the street. "I'll go back with you at"--the latter words, lower spoken, the other did not catch--"no matter what cost!"

Sir Charles dodged a vehicle; he did not observe the light, the fire, the sudden play of fierce, dark passion on his companion's face.

"Good!" he said. "And when you get tired of 'books in the running brooks'--"

Steele's hand closed on his arm. "When do you leave?" he asked abruptly.

"To-day--to-morrow--Suit your convenience."

"Let it be to-day, then! To-day!"

Sir Charles looked at him quickly; John Steele's face recovered its composure.

"I believe I have become weary of what your niece calls the 'dusty byways,'" he explained with a forced laugh.

CHAPTER IX

AWAY FROM THE TOWN

When John Steele, contrary to custom, set aside, in deciding to leave London that day, all logical methods of reasoning and acted on what was nothing more than an irresistible impulse, he did not attempt to belittle to himself the possible consequences that might accrue from his action. He was not following the course intelligence had directed; he was not embarking on a journey his best interests would have prompted; on the contrary, he knew himself mad, foolish. But not for one moment did he regret his decision; stubbornly, obstinately he set his back toward the town; with an enigmatical gleam in his dark eyes he looked away from the blur Sir Charles and he had left behind them.

Green pastures, bright prospects! Whence were they leading him? His gaze was now somber, then bright; though more often shadows passed over his face, like clouds in the sky.

Outwardly his manner had become unconcerned, collected; he listened to Sir Charles' jokes, offered casual comments of his own. He even performed his wonted part in relieving the tedium of a long journey with voluntary contributions to conversations on divers topics in which he displayed wide and far-reaching knowledge. He answered the many questions of his companion on the different habits of criminals; how they lived; the possibilities for reforming the worst of the lot; the various methods toward this end advocated by the idealist. These and other subjects he touched on with poignant, illuminating comment.

Sir Charles regarded him once or twice in surprise. "You have seen a deal in your day," he observed, "of the under world, I mean!" John Steele returned an evasive answer. The nobleman showed a tendency to doze in his seat, despite the jolts and jars of the way, and, thereafter, until they arrived at Strathorn the two fellow travelers rode on in silence.

This little hamlet lay in a sleepy-looking dell; as the driver swung down a hill he whipped up his horses and literally charged upon the town; swept through the main thoroughfare and drew up with a flourish before the principal tavern. Sir Charles started, stretched his legs; John Steele got down.

"Conveyance of any kind here, waiting to take us to Strathorn House?" called out the former as he stiffly descended the ladder at the side of the coach.

The landlord of the Golden Lion, who had emerged from his door, returned an affirmative reply and at the same time ushered the travelers into a tiny private sitting-room. As they crossed the hall, turning to the right to enter this apartment, some one in the room opposite, a more public place, who had been furtively peering through the half-opened door to observe the new-comers, at sight of John Steele drew quickly back. Not, however, before that gentleman had caught a glimpse of him. A strange face, indeed,--but the fellow's manner--his expression--the act itself somehow struck the observer,--unduly, no doubt, and yet--A moment later this door closed, and from beyond came only a murmur of men's voices over pots.

"Trap will be in front directly, Sir Charles," said the landlord lingering. "Meanwhile if there is anything--"

"Nothing, thank you! Only a short distance to Strathorn House," he explained to John Steele, "and I fancy we'll do better by waiting for what we may require there. But what is the latest news at Strathorn? Anything happened? Business quiet?"

"It 'asn't been so brisk, and it 'asn't been so dull, your Lordship, what with now and then a gentleman from London!"

"From London? Isn't that rather unusual?"

"Somewhat. But as for your lordship's first question, I don't know of any news, except Squire Thompson told me to inform your lordship he would have the three hunters he was telling your lordship about, down at his stud farm this afternoon, and if your lordship cared to have a look at them--"

"If?" cried Sir Charles. "There isn't any 'if.' Three finer animals man never threw leg over, judging from report," he explained to John Steele. "Stud farm's about a mile in the opposite direction from Strathorn House. Mind a little jog to the farm first?"

"Not at all!" John Steele had been looking thoughtfully toward the door that had closed upon the man whose quick regard he had detected. "Only, if you will allow me to make a counter proposal,--Strathorn House, you say, is near; I am in the mood for exercise, after sitting so long, and should like to walk there."

"By all means," returned the other, "since it's your preference. Pretty apt to overtake you," he went on, after giving his guest a few directions. "Especially if you linger over any points of interest!"

The trap drew up; the two men separated. Sir Charles rattled briskly down one way, Steele turned to go the other. But before setting out, he asked a casual question or two of the landlord, relating to the occasional "gentleman from London"; the host, however, appeared to know little of any cosmopolitan visitors who had happened to drift that way, and John Steele, eliciting no information in this regard, finally started on his walk. Whatever his thoughts, many quaint and characteristic bits of the town failed to divert them; he looked neither to the right, at a James I. sun-dial; nor to the left, where a small sign proclaimed that an event of historical importance had made noteworthy that particular spot. Over the cobblestones, smoothed by the feet of many generations, he walked with eyes bent straight before him until he reached an open space on the other side of the village, where he paused. On either side hedges partly screened undulating meadows, the broad sweeps of emerald green interspersed here and there with small groups of trees in whose shadows cattle grazed. A stream with lively murmur meandered downward; in a bush, at his approach, a bird began to sing, and involuntarily the man stopped; but only for a moment. Soon rose before him the top of a modest steeple; then a church, within the sanctuary of whose yard old stones mingled with new. He stepped in; "straight on across the churchyard!" had been Sir Charles' direction. John Steele moved quickly down the narrow path; his eye had but time to linger a moment on the monuments, ancient and crumbling, and on headstones more recently fashioned, when above, another picture caught and held his attention.

Strathorn House! A noble dwelling, massive, gray! And yet one that lifted itself with charming lightness from its solid, baronial-like foundation! It adorned the spot, merged into the landscape. Behind, the forest, a dark line, penciled itself against the blue horizon; before the ancient stone pile lay a park. Noble trees guarded the walks, threw over them great gnarled limbs or delicately-trailing branches. Between, the interspaces glowed bright with flowers; amid all, a little lake shone like a silver shield bearing at its center a marble pavilion.

Long the man looked; through a faint veil of mist, turret and tower quivered; strong lines of masonry vibrated. Wavering as in the spell of an optical illusion, the structure might have seemed but a figment of imagination, or one of those fanciful castles sung by the Elizabethan brotherhood of poets. Did the image occur to John Steele, did he feel for the time, despite other disquieting, extraneous thoughts, the subtle enchantment of the scene? The minutes passed; he did not move.

"You find it to your liking?"

A voice, fresh, gay, interrupted; with a great start, he turned.

Jocelyn Wray, for it was she, laughed; so absorbed had he been, he had not heard her light footstep on the grass behind.

"You find it to your liking?" she repeated, tilting quizzically her fair head.

His face changing, "Entirely!" he managed to say. And then, "I--did not know you were near."

"No? But I could see that. Confess," with accent a little derisory, "I startled you." As she spoke she leaned slightly back against the low stone wall of the churchyard; the shifting light through the leaves played over her; her eyes seemed to dance in consonance with that movement.

Illustration: One would have sworn there was joy in her

voice Page

One would have sworn there was joy in her voice Page

"Perhaps," he confessed.

The girl laughed again; one would have sworn there was; oy in her voice. "You must have been much absorbed," she continued, "in the view!"

"It is very fine." He saw now more clearly the picture she made: the details of her dress, the slender figure, closely sheathed in a garb of blue lighter in shade than her eyes.

She put out her hand. "I am forgetting--you came down with my uncle, I suppose?" in a matter-of-fact tone. "A pleasure we hardly expected! Let me see. I haven't seen you since--ah, when was it?"

He told her. "Yes; I remember now. Wasn't that the day the Scotch bagpipes went by? You had business that called you away. Something very important, was it not? You were successful?"

"Quite."

"How oddly you say that!" She looked at him curiously. "But shall we walk on toward the house? I went down into the town thinking to meet my uncle," she explained, "but as I had a few errands, on account of a children's fête we are planning, reached the tavern after he had gone."

"He went to a farm not far distant."

As he spoke, she stepped into the path leading from the churchyard; it was narrow and she walked before him.

"Yes; so the landlord said," she remarked without looking around. And then, irrelevantly, "The others went hunting. Are you a Nimrod, Mr. Steele?"

"Not a mighty one."

"Oh, you wouldn't have to be that--for rabbits!"

She shot a glance over her shoulder; her eyes were glad; but to the man they were bright merely with the joy of youth that drops glances like sunshine for all alike. Perhaps he would have found pleasure in thinking she appeared gayer for sight of him; but if the thought came, bitterly, peremptorily it was dismissed. Sir Charles' words rang through his mind; Lord Ronsdale!--John Steele's hat shaded his eyes; he stopped to pick a small flower from the hedge. When he looked up he saw her face no longer; only the golden hair seemed to flash in his eyes, the beautiful, bright meshes, and the light, slender figure, so graceful, so buoyant, so near he could almost touch it, but moving away, moving from him--

It may be, amid other thoughts, at that moment, he asked himself why he had come. What had driven him to this folly? Why was he stepping on blindly, oblivious of definite plan or policy, like a man walking in the dark? No, not in the dark; all was too bright. He could see but too plainly--her!--felt impelled to draw nearer--

But at that instant, she stepped quickly from the byway into the main road. "There it is," she said, pointing with a small white finger.

He held himself abruptly back. "What?" fell from his lips.

"The way in, of course," said the girl.

He moved now at her side; at the entrance, broad, imposing, she paused; a thousand perfumes seemed wafted from the garden; the rustling of myriad wings fell on the senses, like faint cadences of music. The girl made a courtesy; her red lips curved. "Welcome to Strathorn House, Mr. John Steele!" she said gaily.

Within the stately house, near a recessed window at the front, a man stood at that moment, reading a letter handed to him but a short time before. This document, though brief, was absorbing:

"Shall be down to see you soon. Am sending this by private messenger who may be trusted. Case coming on; links nearly all complete. Involve a new and bewildering possibility that I must impart to you personally. Have discovered the purpose of S.'s visit to the continent. It was--"

Lord Ronsdale perused the words more rapidly; paused, on his face an expression of eagerness, expectancy.

"So that was it," he said to himself slowly. "I might have known--"

Voices without caught his attention; he glanced quickly through the window. Jocelyn Wray and some one else had drawn near, were walking up the marble steps.

"John Steele!" He, Lord Ronsdale, crumpled the paper in his hand. "Here!"

CHAPTER X

A CONTEST

A few days passed; the usual round of pastimes inseparable from house parties served to while away the hours; other guests arrived, one or two went. Lord Ronsdale had greeted John Steele perfunctorily; the other's manner was likewise mechanically courteous. It could not very well have been otherwise; a number of people were near.

"Come down for a little sport?" the nobleman, his hands carelessly thrust into the pockets of his shooting trousers, had asked with a frosty smile.

"Perhaps--if there is any!" Steele allowed his glance for the fraction of a moment to linger on Lord Ronsdale's face.

"I'll answer for that." A slight pause ensued. "Decided rather suddenly to run down, didn't you?"

"Rather."

"Heard you were on the continent. From Sir Charles, don't you know. Pleasant time, I trust?" he drawled.

"Thank you!" John Steele did not answer directly. "Your solicitude," he laughed, "honors me--my Lord!"

And that had been all, all the words spoken, at least. To the others there had been nothing beneath the surface between them; for the time the two men constituted but two figures in a social gathering.

A rainy spell put a stop to outdoor diversions; for twenty-four hours now the party had been thrown upon their own resources, to devise such indoor amusement as occurred to them. Strathorn House, however, was large; it had its concert stage, a modern innovation; its armory hall and its ball-room. Pleasure seekers could and did find here ample facilities for entertaining themselves.

The second morning of the dark weather discovered two of the guests in the oak-paneled smoking-room of Strathorn House. One of them brushed the ash from his cigar meditatively and then stretched himself more comfortably in the great leather chair.

"No fox-hunt or fishing for any of us to-day," he remarked with a yawn.

The other, who had been gazing through a window at a prospect of dripping leaves and leaden sky, answered absently; then his attention centered itself on the small figure of a boy coming up through the avenue of trees toward a side entrance.

"Believe I shall run over to Germany very soon, Steele," went on the first speaker.

"Indeed?" John Steele's brows drew together; the appearance of the lad was vaguely familiar. He remembered him now, the hostler boy at the Golden Lion.

"Yes; capital case coming on in the criminal courts there."

"And you don't want to miss it, Forsythe?"

"Not I! Weakness of mine, as you know. Most people look to novels or plays for entertainment; I find mine in the real drama, unfolded every day in the courts of justice."

Forsythe paused as if waiting for some comment from his companion, but none came. John Steele watched the boy; he waved a paper in his hand and called with easy familiarity to a housemaid in an open window above:

"Telegram from London, Miss. My master at the Golden Lion said there'd be a sixpence here for delivering it!"

"Well, I'll be down in a moment, Impudence."

The silence that followed was again broken by Captain Forsythe's voice: "There are one or two features in this German affair that remind me of another case, some years back--one of our own--that interested me."

"Ah?" The listener's tone was only politely interrogatory.

"A case here in London--perhaps you have heard of it? The murder of a woman, once well-known before the footlights, by a one-time champion of the ring--the 'Frisco Pet, I think he was called."

The other moved slightly; his back had been toward Forsythe; he now half-turned. "Yea, I have heard of it," he said slowly, after a pause. "But why should this case across the water interest you; because it is like--this other one you mention?"

"Because I once puzzled a bit over that one; investigated it somewhat on my own account, don't you know."

"In what way?" Steele's manner was no longer indifferent. "I'm rather familiar with some of the details myself," he added.

"Then it attracted you, too, as an investigator?" murmured the captain in a gratified tone. "For your book, perhaps?"

"Not exactly. But you haven't yet told me," in a keen, alert tone, "why you looked into it, 'on your own account.' It seems simple, obvious. Not of the kind that would attract one fond of nice criminal problems."

"That is just it," said Captain Forsythe, rising. "It was, perhaps, a little too simple! too obvious."

"How," demanded John Steele, "can a matter of this sort be too obvious? But," bending his eyes on the other, "you attended the trial of this fellow?" His tone vibrated a little oddly.

"The last part of it; wasn't in England when it first came on; and what I heard of it raised some questions and doubts in my mind. Not that I haven't the greatest respect for English justice! However, I didn't think much more about the case until a good many months later, when chance alone drew my attention more closely to it."

"Chance?"

"Was down in the country--jolly good trout district--when one night, while riding my favorite hobby, I happened to get on this almost-forgotten case of the 'Frisco Pet. Whereupon the landlord of the inn where I put up, informed me that one of the villagers in this identical little town had been landlady at the place where the affair occurred."

"The woman who testified no one had been to her place that night except--" John Steele spoke sharply.

"This fellow? Quite so." Captain Forsythe walked up and down. "Now, I'd always had a little theory. Could never get out of my mind one sentence this poor, ignorant fellow uttered at the trial. 'Seems as if I could remember a man's face, a stranger's, that looked into mine that night, your Lordship, but I ain't exactly cock-sure!' 'Ain't exactly cock-sure,'" repeated Captain Forsythe. "That's what caught me. Would a man, not telling the truth, be not quite 'cock-sure'; or would he testify to the face as a fact?" The other did not answer. "So the impression grew on me. Can you understand?"

"Hum! Very interesting, Forsythe; very ingenious; quite plausible!"

"Now you're laughing at me, Steele?"

"On the contrary, my dear fellow, go on."

"The landlady's testimony excluded the face, made it a figment of an imagination, disordered by drink!" Captain Forsythe waved his hand airily as he stepped back and forth.

"You went to see this woman?"

"Out of curiosity, and found she was, indeed, the same person. She seemed quite ill and feeble; I talked with her about an hour that day. Tried in every way to get her to remember she had possibly let in some other person that night, but--"

"But?"

"Bless you, she stuck to her story," laughed Captain Forsythe. "Couldn't move her an iota." One of the listener's arms fell to his side; his hand closed hard. "Quite bowled over my little theory, don't you know! Of course I told myself it didn't matter; the man convicted was gone, drowned. However,--" he broke off. A swish of silk was heard in the hallway; Forsythe stopped before the door.

"Ah, Miss Jocelyn! Haven't you a word in passing?"

She paused, looked in. Amid neutral shades the girl's slender figure shone most insistent; her gown, of a color between rose and pink, was warm-hued rather than bright, like the tints in an ancient embroidery. Around her neck gleamed a band of old cloth of silver but the warmth of tone did not cease at the argent edge, but leaped over to kiss the fair cheeks and soft, smiling lips. "Is this the way you men amuse yourselves?" she asked with a laugh. "Talking shop, no doubt?"

"Afraid we must plead guilty," said Captain Forsythe.

"And that is why," with a quick sidelong glance, drawing her skirts around her as she stood gracefully poised, "Mr. Steele appears so interested?"

"Interested?" The subject of her comment seemed to pull himself together with a start, regarded her. Was he, in the surprise of the moment, just in the least disconcerted by that bright presence, the beautiful clear eyes, straight, direct, though laughing? "Perhaps appearances are--" he found himself saying.

"Deceptive!" she completed lightly. "Well, if you weren't interested, Captain Forsythe was. He, I know, is quite incorrigible when you get him on his hobby."

"Oh, I say, Miss Jocelyn!"

She came forward; light and brightness entered the room with her. "Quite!" The slender figure stood between the two men. "We expect any time he'll be looking around here next, to find something to investigate!"

"Here?" John Steele smiled. "What should he find here?"

"In sleepy Strathorn? True!"

A shrill whistle smote the air; Steele's glance turned to the window. The boy, having delivered his message, had left the door; with lips puckered to the loud and imperfect rendition of a popular street melody, he was making his way through the grounds. Involuntarily the man's look lingered on him. "A telegram from London? For whom?"

"I'm afraid it's hopeless, Captain Forsythe. Nothing ever happens at Strathorn." At the instant the girl's laughing voice seemed a little farther off. "If something only would--to help pass the time. Don't you agree with me, Mr. Steele?"

"I--" his glance returned to her quickly, "by all means!"

She looked at him; had she detected that momentary swerving from the serious consideration of her light words? Her own eyes turned to the window where they saw nothing but rain. She smiled vaguely, stood with her hands behind her; it was he now who regarded her, straight, slender, lithe. There was also something inflexible appearing in that young form, though so replete with grace and charm.

"To help pass the time!" John Steele laughed. "I--let us hope so."

There had been moments in the past when she had felt she could not quite understand him; they were moments like these when she seemed to become aware of something obscuring, falling before her--between them--that seemed to hold him aloof from her, from the others, to invest him almost with mystery. Mystery,--romantic idea! A slight laugh welled from the white throat. In these prosaic days!

"By the way, what particular case were you discussing when I happened by?"

"Nothing very new," answered the military man, "an old crime perpetrated by a fellow called the--"

"Beg pardon!" A footman stood in the doorway. "Sir Charles' compliments to the gentlemen, and will they be good enough to join him in armory hall?"

John Steele turned quickly to the servant, so quickly a close observer might have fancied he welcomed the interruption. "Captain Forsythe's and Mr. Steele's compliments to Sir Charles," he said at once, "and say it will give them pleasure to comply. That is," he added, bowing, "with your permission, Miss Wray."

She assented lightly; preceded by the girl, the two men left the room and mounted the broad stairway leading to the second story.

Armory hall was a large and lofty chamber with vaulted ceiling, that dated back almost to the early Norman period; its walls, decorated in geometrical designs, were covered with many varieties of antique weapons of warfare; halberd and mace gleamed and mingled with harquebus, poleax or lance. At one end of the hall were ranged in a row suits of armor which at first glance looked like real knights, drawn up in company front; then the empty helmets dawned on the beholder, transforming them into mere vacuous relics.

As Steele and his companion together with Jocelyn Wray entered, sounds of merriment and applause greeted the ear; two men in fencing array who had apparently just ended a match were the center of an animated company.

"A little contest with the foils! A fencing bout! Good!" exclaimed Forsythe.

Jocelyn Wray walked over to the group and Forsythe followed.

"Bravo, Ronsdale!" A number of people applauded.

"He has won. Now the reward! What is it to be?"

"Not so fast! Here are others."

"True!" Ronsdale looked around with his cold smile; his glance vaguely included John Steele and Captain Forsythe.

"Count me out!" laughed the latter. "Not in my line, don't you know, since I joined the retired list!"

"However, there's Steele," Sir Charles, pipe in hand, remarked.

Ronsdale had stepped to the girl's side; his eyes, regarding her in the least degree too steadily, shone with a warmer gleam. She appeared either not to notice, or to mind; with look unreservedly bright, she smiled back at him; then her gaze met John Steele's.

"Do you use the foils, Mr. Steele?"

He moved forward; Lord Ronsdale stood near her, bending over with a slightly proprietary air.

"I--" Steele looked at them, at the girl's questioning eyes. "Only a little!"

"Then you must try conclusions with Lord Ronsdale!" called out Sir Charles. "As victor over the rest he must meet all comers."

A light swept John Steele's face; perhaps the situation appealed to a certain sense of humor; he hesitated.

"Nothing to be put out by, being beaten by Ronsdale," interposed an observer. "Had the reputation of being one of the best swordsmen on the continent; has even had, I believe," with a laugh, "one or two little affairs of honor."

"Honor!" Steele's glance swung around, played brightly on the nobleman.

The latter's face remained impassive; he lifted his foil carelessly and swung it; the hiss that followed might have been construed as a challenge. John Steele tossed aside his coat.

"Can't promise this contest will be as interesting as the other little affairs you speak of!" he laughed. Through the fine, white linen of his shirt could be discerned the superb swell and molding of the muscles, as he now, with the gleaming toy in hand, stood before Ronsdale.

The latter's eyes suddenly narrowed; a covert expectancy made itself felt in his manner. "Aren't you going to roll up your sleeve?" he asked softly. "Usually find it gives greater freedom of movement, myself."

Steele did not at once reply; in his eyes bent on Ronsdale a question seemed to flash; then a bolder, more daring light replaced it. "Perhaps you are right!" he said coolly, and following the nobleman's example he pushed back his sleeve. The action revealed the splendid arm of the perfectly-trained athlete marked, however, by a great scar extending from just above the wrist to the elbow. Lord Ronsdale's eyes fastened on it; his lips moved slightly but if any sound fell from them, it was rendered inaudible by Sir Charles' exclamation:

"Bad jab, that, Steele! Looks as if it might have been made by an African spear!"

"No." John Steele smiled, encountering other glances, curious, questioning. "Can't include the land of ivory among the countries I've been in," he added easily.

Lord Ronsdale breathed quickly. "Recent wound, I should say."

"Not very old," said John Steele.

"If there's a good story back of it, we'll have it later," Captain Forsythe remarked.

"Perhaps Mr. Steele is too modest to tell it," Ronsdale again interposed.

"Your good opinion flatters me." Steele's eyes met the other's squarely; then he made a brusk movement. "But if you are ready?"

Their blades crossed. Ronsdale's suppleness of wrist and arm, his cold steadiness, combined with a knowledge of many fine artifices, had already made him a favorite with those of the men who cared to back their opinions with odd pounds. As he pressed his advantage, the girl's eyes turned to John Steele; her look seemed to express just a shade of disappointment. His manner, or method, appeared perfunctory, too perfunctory! Why did he not enter into the contest with more abandon? Between flashes of steel she again saw the scar on his arm; it seemed to exercise a sort of fascination over her.

What had caused it, this jagged, irregular mark? He had not said. Lord Ronsdale's words, "A recent wound--perhaps Mr. Steele is too modest--" returned to her. It was not so much the words as the tone, an inflection almost too fine to notice, a covert sneer. Or, was it that? Her brows drew together slightly. Of course not. And yet she felt vaguely puzzled, as if some fine instinct in her divined something, she knew not what, beneath the surface. Absurd! Her eyes at that moment met John Steele's. Did he read, guess what was passing through her brain? An instant's carelessness nearly cost him the match.

"Ten to five!" one of the men near her called out jovially. "Odds on Ronsdale! Any takers?"

"Done!"

She saw John Steele draw himself back sharply just in time; she also fancied a new, ominous gleam in his eyes. His demeanor underwent an abrupt change. If Ronsdale's quickness was cat-like, the other's movements had now all the swiftness and grace of a panther. The girl's eyes widened; all vague questioning vanished straightway from her mind; it was certainly very beautiful, that agility, that deft, incessant wrist play.

"Hello!" Through the swishing of steel she heard again the man at her side exclaim, make some laughing remark: "Perhaps I'd better hedge--"

But even as he spoke, with a fiercer thrusting and parrying of blades the end came; a sudden irresistible movement of John Steele's arm, and the nobleman's blade clattered to the floor.

"Egad! I never saw anything prettier!" Sir Charles came forward quickly. "Met your match that time, Ronsdale," in a tone the least bantering.

The nobleman stooped for his foil. "That time, yes!" he drawled. If he felt chagrin, or annoyance, he concealed it.

"Lucky it wasn't one of those real affairs of honor, eh?" some one whom Ronsdale had defeated laughed good-naturedly.

Again he replied. Steele found himself walking with Jocelyn Wray toward the window. Across the room a footman who had been waiting for the conclusion of the contest, and an opportune moment, now approached Lord Ronsdale and extended a salver.

"It came a short time ago, my Lord!"

John Steele heard; his glance flashed toward Ronsdale. The telegram, then, had been for--? He saw an inscrutable smile cross the nobleman's face.

"Any more aspirants?" the military man called out.

"Only myself left," observed Sir Charles. "And I resign the privilege!"

"Then," said the girl, standing somewhat apart with John Steele, near one of the great open windows, "must you, Mr. Steele, be proclaimed victor?"

"Victor!" He looked down. Between them bright colors danced, reflections of hues from the old stained glass above; they shone like red roses fallen from her lap at his feet. For a moment he continued to regard them; then slowly gazed up to the soft colored gown, to the beautiful young face, the hair that shone brightly against the background of branches and twigs, gleaming with watery drops like thousands of gems. "Victor!" He--

A door closed quietly as Lord Ronsdale went out.

CHAPTER XI

WAYS AND MEANS

The afternoon of that same day there arrived at the village of Strathorn from London a discreet-looking little man who, descending at the Golden Lion, was shown to a private sitting-room on the second story. Calling for a half-pint from the best tap and casually surveying the room, he settled himself in a chair with an air of nonchalance, which a certain eagerness in his eyes seemed to belie.

"Any mail or message for me, landlord?" he inquired, giving his name, when that worthy reappeared with the tankard.

"No, sir."

"Nor any callers?"

"None that I've heard of--" A sound of wheels at that moment interrupted; the landlord went to the window. "Why, it's his lordship," he remarked. "And such weather to be out in!" as a sudden gust of rain beat against the pane. "Lord Ronsdale who is staying at Strathorn House," he explained for the stranger's benefit. "And he's coming in!"

The host hurried to the door but already a footstep was heard on the stairway and the voice of the nobleman inquiring for the new-comer's room.

"Right up this way! The gentleman is in here, your Lordship," called down the landlord. Lord Ronsdale mounted leisurely and entered the room.

"I didn't expect to have the honor of a call from your lordship," said the guest of the Golden Lion, bowing low. "If your lordship had indicated to me his pleasure--"

The nobleman whipped a greatcoat from his shoulders and tossed it to the landlord. "Was coming to the village on another little matter, and thought I might as well drop in and see you," he observed to the guest, "instead of waiting for you to come to Strathorn House. You have the stock-lists and market prices with you?" he queried meaningly. The other answered in the affirmative. "Very good, we will consider the matter, and--you may go, landlord."

But when the innkeeper had taken his departure no further word was said by the nobleman of securities or values; Lord Ronsdale gazed keenly at his companion. Without, the wind swept drearily down the little winding street, and sighed about the broad overhanging eaves.

"Well," he spoke quickly, "I fancy you have a little something to tell me, Mr. Gillett?"

"'A little something?'" The latter rubbed his hands. "More than a little! Your lordship little dreamed, when--"

"Spare me your observations," broke in the nobleman. "Come at once to the business on hand." His voice, though low, had a strident pitch; behind it might be fancied strained nerves.

"As your lordship knows, good fortune or chance favored me at the start; that is, along one line, the line of general investigation. The special inquiry which your lordship mentioned, just as he was leaving my office, proved for a time most illusive."

"You mean the object of John Steele's visit to the continent?"

"Exactly. And the object of that visit solved, I have now a matter of greatest importance to communicate, so important it could only be imparted by word of mouth!" The police agent spoke hastily and moved nearer.

"Indeed?" Lord Ronsdale's thin, cold lips raised slightly, but not to suggest a smile; his eyes met the police agent's. "You have reached a conclusion? One that you sought to reject, perhaps, but that wouldn't be discarded?"

Mr. Gillett looked at him earnestly. "You don't mean--it isn't possible that you knew all the while--?"

The white, aristocratic hand of Lord Ronsdale waved. "Let us start at the beginning."

"True, your Lordship," Mr. Gillett swallowed. "As your lordship is aware, we were fortunate enough in the beginning to find out through our agent in Tasmania that John Steele came to that place in a little trading schooner, the Laura Deane, of Portsmouth; that he had been rescued from a tiny uncharted reef, or isle, on December twenty-first, some three years before. The spot, by longitude and latitude, marks, through an odd coincidence, the place where the Lord Nelson met her fate."

"A coincidence truly," murmured the nobleman. "But at this stage in your reasoning you recalled that all on board were embarked in the ships' boats and reached civilization, except possibly--"

"A few of my charges between decks? True; I remembered that. A bad lot of ugly brutes!" Mr. Gillett paused; Lord Ronsdale raised his head. "The story of John Steele's rescue," went on Mr. Gillett, "as told by himself," significantly, "was well known in Tasmania and not hard to learn. A man of splendid intellect, a lawyer by profession, he had been passenger on a merchant vessel, the Mary Vernon, of Baltimore, United States. This vessel, like the Lord Nelson, had come to grief; after being tossed about, a helpless, water-logged wreck, it had finally been abandoned. All of those in John Steele's boat had perished except him; some had gone mad through thirst and suffering; others had killed their fellows in a frenzy. Being of superb physique, having been through much physical training--" the listener stirred in his chair--"he managed to survive, to reach the little isle, where, according to his story, he remained almost a year."

"A year? Then he set foot in Tasmania about four years after the Lord Nelson went down," observed the nobleman, a curious glitter in his eyes. "Four years after," he repeated, accenting the last word.

"Such were the details gathered in Tasmania," answered the police agent.

"Go on," said Lord Ronsdale. "You subsequently learned with more definiteness the actual circumstances of his rescue?"

"From the mate of the Laura Deane, the schooner that rescued him from the isle, and one of her crew whom I managed to locate at Plymouth, as I have informed your lordship by letter," answered Mr. Gillett. "These men now furnish lodgings to seamen, and incidentally shanghai a few of them for dubious craft! Both of them, the mate and the sailor, recalled the man of fine bearing and education whom they found on the little isle, a sort of Greek statue, half-clothed in rags, so to speak, who made his personality felt at once on these simple, ignorant fellows!" Mr. Gillett paused to look at Lord Ronsdale, seemed waiting for the latter to say something, but the nobleman only leaned forward and pushed at the coals with a poker.

"Which brings to my mind the one point," with emphasis, "that I haven't been able so far to reconcile or to explain. Your lordship, who seems to have divined a great deal, can, perhaps. A man of fine education and bearing, as I said, yet the other had been--"

"It is your business, not mine, to explain," interrupted the listener. "Tell all you know."

"At the spring on the little island the seamen filled their water-butts; this kept them several days, mixing labor with skylarking, during which time one of them picked up something, a pouch marked with a name."

"Which was--?"

Mr. Gillett leaned forward, spoke softly; Lord Ronsdale stared straight ahead. "Of course," he said, "of course!"

"This, I will confess, startled, puzzled me," continued the police agent after a pause. "What did it mean? I tried to explain it in a dozen different ways but none of them seemed exactly to fit. Then it was that the line of special investigation helped. John Steele's outing to which you directed my attention was passed on the continent. What did he do there; was it business; was it pleasure took him there? After a good deal of pains, we discovered that he visited a certain large building, centrally located. This proved a starting-point; why did he go there? At the top was a studio; from the concierge we learned that he had asked for the artist. From the artist we ascertained that John Steele had bought a picture; that he had called several times to watch the painter at his work. So far, so good, or bad! For was it likely John Steele had come to Paris to buy a bit of canvas, or was his interest in art assumed to cover his real purpose? When he left the studio, did he, without the knowledge of the concierge, call on some one else in the building?

"This thought led to an inspection of the tenants. They proved of all sorts and kinds; the place was a beehive; hundreds of people entered and left every day. At this time I happened on an item in a periodical about some remarkable work in a certain line by a high-class medical specialist. Here is the paragraph."

Lord Ronsdale took the slip of paper the other handed him and briefly looked at it. "You visited this person?"

"Yes, as his office address was mentioned as being in the large building we were interested in. But at the moment I had no suspicion that John Steele's pilgrimage to Paris could have been for the purpose of consulting,--"

"An eminent specialist in the line of removing birth-marks," glancing at the slip of paper, "or other disfigurements--"

"Such as I described to your lordship from the book that day in the office," murmured the police agent.

For some moments both were again silent; only the sounds of the wind and the rain, mingled with monotonous creakings, broke the stillness.

"You say this shipwrecked man was like a Greek statue, half clothed in rags. Perhaps then," slowly, "since he was only half-clothed the rescuers might have noticed--"

"I sought them at once," with sudden eagerness, "to verify what your lordship suggests, and I have their full corroboration; what the evidence of their eyes told them, that the rescued man bore on his arm the exact markings described in my book."

"A coincidence not easily accounted for." The speaker's tones had a rasping sound. "And now--"

"One question, my Lord. He is discerning--knows that you--"

"Knows? Yes; he found that out one day in Hyde Park, never mind how; about the same time I, too, learned something."

"And yet he deliberately comes down here, dares to leave London where at least his chances are better for--but why? It is unreasonable; I don't understand."

"Why?" Lord Ronsdale's smile was not agreeable. "When does a man become illogical, stray from the path good reasoning should keep him in? When does he accept chances, however desperate?"

"When?" The police agent's tones expressed vague wonder. "Why, when-- there is a woman in the case!" suddenly.

"A woman, or a girl."

"Your lordship means--"

"One who is beautiful enough to enmesh any man's fancy," he spoke as to himself, "whose golden hair is a web to draw lovers like the fleece of old; whose eyes like the sunny heavens tempt them to bask in their light."

The words were mocking yet seemed to force themselves from his lips. "When you add that she has high position; is as opulent in the world's goods as she is rich in personal--" abruptly he paused. "But this is irrelevant," he added almost angrily. "Is there anything else you have to tell me?"

"Only one thing, and it may have no bearing on the case; some one who has not been seen in these parts in years, the red-headed son of the landlady where the Gerard murder occurred has been back in London, and--Steele's been looking for him. For what purpose, I don't know." The nobleman moved quickly. "But he hasn't found him--yet; apparently the fellow took alarm, knowing the police agent might want him, and vanished again."

Lord Ronsdale moistened his lips; then got up, walked back and forth. A brisker gust, without, and the tin symbol of the Golden Lion over the

entrance to the inn swung with a harsh rattle almost around the bar that
held it. The nobleman stopped short; from the dim corner where he stood
his eyes gleamed with animal brightness.

"And now?" suggested Mr. Gillett. "Your lordship of course knows what this
means, if your lordship uses the weapons you have in your hands? The
penalty for one transported returning to England is--"

"I know," interrupted the other. "He has, however, dared to come back, to
incur that risk. Any plea he could hope to make," Lord Ronsdale spoke with
studied deliberation, "to justify the act, he could not--substantiate." The
speaker lingered on the word then went on more crisply. "He stands in the
position of a person who has broken one of the most exacting laws of the
realm and one which has on all occasions been rigorously enforced. He has
presumed to trespass in the highest circles, to mingle with people of rank,
our gentry, our ladies--"

"Then your lordship will--"

"I have made my plans. And--I intend to act."

"Where?"

"Here."

"But would it not be better to wait until he returns to London, my Lord?"

"And give him more time to--" he broke off. "We act here, at once!"

Lord Ronsdale again seated himself; his face had regained its hard mask; he
motioned the other man to draw his chair closer. "I'll tell you how to
proceed."

CHAPTER XII

FESTIVITIES

The windows in Strathorn House shone bright; from within came the sound of music; in the billiard room, adjoining the spacious hall, a number of persons were smoking, playing, or watching the dancers. At one of the tables two men had about finished a game; by the skilful stroke of him who showed the better score, the balls clicked briskly, separated, and came together once more.

"Enough to go out with!" The player, Captain Forsythe, counted his score. "Shall we say another, Steele?"

"Not for me!" John Steele placed his cue in the rack. "I'm out for a breath of air." And he stepped through an open French window, leading upon a balcony that almost spanned the rear of the house.

"Mr. Steele seems to be rather out of form to-night." A plump, short woman with doll-like eyes, who had been watching the game from a seat near-by, now spoke, with subtle meaning in her accents.

"Quite so. Can't really understand it. Steele can put up a deuced strong game, don't you know, but to-night--Did you notice how he failed at one of the easiest shots?"

"That was when Jocelyn Wray looked in," murmured the other.

"Miss Wray!" Captain Forsythe set the balls for a practice shot. "Well, Steele's a splendid chap," he said irrelevantly.

"You have known him for some time?"

"Not a great while; he's rather a new man, don't you know. But Sir Charles is quite democratic; took him up, well, as one might in Australia, without," good-naturedly, "inquiring into his family or his antecedents, or all that sort of rubbish."

"Indeed?" Her voice was non-committal. "But as for its being rubbish--"

"Oh, I say, Mrs. Nallis!" The other's tone was expostulating. "Strong man; splendid sort of chap, Steele! A jolly good athlete, too! Witness our little fencing contest of this morning!"

"True! You are an evident admirer of Mr. Steele, Captain Forsythe. And if I am not mistaken," she laughed, "others share your opinion. Sir Charles, for example, and Jocelyn Wray. She didn't look displeased this morning, did she? When the contest was over, I mean. Not that I would imply--of course, her position and his--so far apart from a social standpoint." A retort of some kind seemed about to spring from the listener's lips but she did not give him the opportunity to speak; went on: "Besides, when I came here, I understood a marriage had been, or was about to be arranged between Sir Charles' niece and--"

"Not interrupting a bit of gossip, I trust?" a cynical voice inquired; at the same time a third person, who had quietly approached, paused to regard them.

"Ah, Lord Ronsdale!" Just for an instant the lady was disconcerted. "Gossip?" She repeated in a tone that meant: "How can you?"

He waved his hand; leaned against the table. "Beg your pardon! Very wrong of me, no doubt; only the truth is--" his lashes drooped slightly to veil his eyes, "I like a bit of gossip myself occasionally!"

"We were talking about your friendly set-to with John Steele," said Captain Forsythe bluntly.

The nobleman's long fingers lifted, pulled at his mustache; in the bright glare, his nails, perfectly kept, looked sharp and pointed. "Ah, indeed!" he remarked. "Steele is handy with the foils; an all-round sportsman, I fancy; or once was!" softly.

"Never heard of him, though, in the amateur sporting world!" observed the lady. "Never saw his name mentioned in any gentlemen's events--tennis or golf tournaments, track athletics, rowing, and all that."

"No?" Lord Ronsdale gazed down; half-sitting on the corner of the table, he swung one glossy shoe to and fro.

"Perhaps he's hiding his light under a bushel?" said the lady.

The nobleman made a sound. "Perhaps!"

"I was asking Captain Forsythe about his antecedents. No one here seems to know. Possibly you can enlighten us."

"I?" Lord Ronsdale's tone was purring. "Why should I be able to? But I see Miss Wray," rising and walking toward the door. "My dance, don't you know."

She gazed after him. "I wonder why Lord Ronsdale does not approve of, or shall we say, dislikes Mr. John Steele?"

"Eh?--what?--I never noticed."

"A man notice?" She laughed. "But your game of billiards? You are looking for some one. If I will do--?"

"Delighted!" he Said with an accent of reserve.

Meanwhile the principal subject of this conversation had been walking slowly on the broad stone balcony toward the ball-room; there he had stopped; then stepping to the balustrade, he stood looking off. The night was warm; in the sky, stars seemed trying to maintain their places between dark, floating clouds. Near at hand the foliage shimmered with pale flashes of light; the perfumes of dew-laden flowers were like those of an oriental bower. Faint rustlings, soft undertones broke upon the ear from dark places; mists seemed drawn like phantom ribbons, now here, now there. He looked at the stars; watched one of them, very small, drop into the maw of a black-looking monster of vapor. As it vanished the sound of music was wafted from within; John Steele listened; they were beginning once more to dance.

He glanced around; splashes of color met the eye; hues that shifted, mingled; came swiftly and went. In the great hall, staring Lelys and Knellers looked down from their high, gilded frames; the glaring lights of a great crystal chandelier threw a flood of rays over the scene at once brilliant and dazzling. Steele stepped toward the window, paused; his eyes seemed searching the throng. They found what they sought, a slender, erect form, the gown soft, white, like foam; a face, animated, joyous. For an instant only, however, he saw the beautiful features; then as Jocelyn turned in the dance, around her waist glimpsed a black band, tipped by slender masculine fingers; above, a cynical countenance. Or was it all cynical now? A brief glance showed more than the habitual expression, a sedulousness-- some passionate feeling? Lord Ronsdale's look seemed once more to say he held and claimed her; that she was his, or soon would be.

A fleeting picture; she was gone and other figures intervened. John Steele stood with hands tightly clasped. Then his gaze gradually lowered; he moved restlessly back and forth; but the music sounded louder and he walked away from it, to the end of the balcony and again looked off--into darkness.

The moments passed; a distant buzz replaced melody; the human murmur, the scraping of strings. From the forest came a far-away cry, the melancholy sound of some wood-creature. He continued motionless, suddenly wheeled swiftly.

"That is you, Mr. Steele?" A voice, young, gay, sounded near; Jocelyn Wray came toward him; from her shoulders floated a white scarf. "You have come out for the freshness of the garden? Although," she added, "you shouldn't altogether seclude yourself from the madding crowd."

"No?" In the eyes that met hers flashed a question, the question that he had ever been asking himself since coming to Strathorn House, that had driven him there.

Did she note the strangeness of the look she seemed to have surprised on his face? Her own glance grew on the instant slightly puzzled, showed a passing constraint; then her manner became light again. "No. Especially as-- You are leaving to-morrow, I believe?"

"Yes." He tried to speak in conventional tones; but his gaze swerved from the graceful figure with its dim, white lines that changed and fluttered in the faint breath of air, stealing so gently by them and away. "My time is almost up; the allotted period of my brief Elysium!" he half-laughed.

"And yet it was rather hard to get you here, wasn't it? You remember you quite scorned our first invitation," gaily.

"Scorned?" In the semi-darkness he could only divine her features. "That is hardly the word."

"Isn't it? Well, then, you had business more important," she laughed.

"Not more important,--imperative." Was his voice, beneath an assumption of carelessness, just a shade uncertain? again it became conventional. "I--have enjoyed myself immensely."

"Have you?" She glanced at him; a flicker of light touched the strong face. "So good of you to say so! I believe that answer is the proper formula. Invented by our ancestors," lightly, "and handed down!"

He did not at once reply; again she caught a suggestion of that searching look she had noted before, and after a moment the girl turned; walking to a rose-bush that partly screened one end of the balcony, she bent over the flowers. "Of course I might use my influence with my aunt to have the time allotted you, as you put it, extended. Especially as you are so appreciative!" she laughed. "Until after the children's fête, for example! What do you say? Shall I plead for you until then? If you will promise to make yourself very useful!"

"I--you are very good--but--"

"Don't!" She spread out her hands. "Forgive me for presuming to think that Strathorn House and its poor attractions could longer keep Mr. John Steele from smoky London-town and the drone of its courts!"

"It is not that"--he began, stopped.

"Go; we abandon you to your fate." It may be that he had made her feel she had been somewhat over gracious, as he had, once or twice before,--that night at the opera, when they had first met; afterward on taking leave of him on the return from Hyde Park. But she only laughed again, perhaps a little constrainedly this time. "You will miss the revival of a few old rural pastimes!" she went on. "That sounds quite trivial to you though, does it not? Several of our present guests will stay, however; others are coming; Lord Ronsdale," lightly, "has even begged to remain; we shall probably lead the old country-dance."

"Lord Ronsdale!--You!"--The flame again played in the dark eyes, more strongly now, no longer to be suppressed.

"Mr. Steele!" Her brows arched in sudden surprise; she drew back a little.

He seemed about to speak but with an effort checked himself and looked down. "I beg your pardon." His face was half-turned; for a moment he did not go on. "I beg your pardon." He again raised his head; his face was steady, very steady now; his words too. "Your mentioning Lord Ronsdale reminded me of a social obligation; which I have neglected, or forgotten; the pleasure," with a slight laugh, "of congratulating you--is that the word? Or Lord Ronsdale,--he, I believe, is the one to be congratulated!"

"Congratulated?" Her face had changed, grown colder. His hand grasped the stone balustrade, but he forced a smile to his lips. "I can not imagine who has started--why you speak thus. Lord Ronsdale is an old friend of my uncle, and--mine, too. But that is all; I am not--have not been. You are mistaken."

"Mistaken?" The word broke from him quickly; the strained expression of his face gave way to another he could ill conceal. Before the light in his gaze, the fire, the ardency, her own slowly fell; she turned slightly as if to go. But he made no effort to stop her, spoke no word. She took a step, hesitated; John Steele moved.

"Good-by," he said slowly. "I am leaving rather early in the morning; I shall not see you again."

"Good-by." She raised her head with outward assurance. "At least until we meet in London," she ended lightly.

"That may not be--"

"Why, you are not thinking of leaving London?" with gaiety perhaps a trifle forced, "of deserting your dingy metropolis?"

He did not answer; she looked at him quickly; something in his face held her; a little of the lightness went from hers.

"Once more, good-by, Miss--Jocelyn."

His look was now resolute; but his voice lingered on her name. He extended his hand in the matter-of-fact manner of one who knew very well what he had to do; the girl's eyes widened on him. Did she realize he was saying "Good-by" to her for all time? She held her head higher, pressed her lips slightly closer. Then she sought to withdraw her hand but he, as hardly knowing what he did, or yielding to sudden, irresistible temptation, clasped for an instant the slim fingers closer; they seemed to quiver in his. The girl's figure moved somewhat from him; she stood almost amid the roses, dark spots that nodded around her. The bush was a mass of bloom; did she tremble ever so slightly? Or was it but the fine, sensitive petals behind her that stirred when kissed by the sweet-scented breeze?

John Steele breathed deeply; he continued to regard her, so fair, so beautiful! A leaf fell; she made a movement; it seemed to awaken him to realization. He started and threw back his head; the dark, glowing eyes became once more resolute. An instant, and he bent; a breath, or his lips, swept the delicate, white fingers; then he dropped them. Her hand swung back against the cold stone; on her breast, something bright--an ornament-- fluttered, became still. Behind, a bird chirped; her glance turned toward the ball-room.

"I--"

Other voices, loud, merry, coming from one of the open French windows interrupted.

"Jocelyn!" They called to her; faces looked out. "Jocelyn!"

"Yes!" She was walking rapidly from him now, a laugh, a little forced, on her lips.

On the balcony a number of persons appeared. "A cotillion! We're going to have a cotillion; that is, if you--"

"Of course, if you wish." The gay group surrounded her; light, heedless voices mingled; then she, all of them, vanished into the ball-room.

John Steele moved slowly down the stone steps leading to the garden below. One thought vibrated in his mind. Sir Charles had erred when he told him that day in the park of his niece and Ronsdale. Perhaps because the wish was father to the thought--But the girl's own assurance dispelled all doubts and fears. He, John Steele, had been mistaken. Those were her words, "Mistaken!"

He could go away now, gladly, gladly! No; not that, perhaps; but he could go. If need be,--far from England; never to be seen, heard of, more by her. He could go, and she would never know she had honored by her friendship, had sheltered beneath her roof, one who--As he walked down the dimly lighted path somebody--a man--standing under the trees, at one side, at that moment touched his arm.

"I should like to speak with you, sir!" said a voice, and turning with a quick jerk, Steele saw the familiar features of Gillett, the former police agent; behind him, other men.

"What do you want?"

The Scotland Yard man coughed significantly. "Out here is a nice, quiet place for a word, or so," he said in his blandest manner. "And if you will be so good--"

John Steele's reply was as emphatic as it was sudden; he had been dreaming; the awakening had come. A glint like lightning flashed from his eyes; well, here was something tangible to be grappled with! A laugh burst from his throat; with the quickness of thought he launched himself forward.

CHAPTER XIII

THE PRINCESS SUITE

A House maid, some time later that night, moved noiselessly over the heavy rugs in the boudoir of the princess suite, next to armory hall on the second story of Strathorn House. Glancing nervously about her from time to time, the woman trimmed a candle here and set another there; then lifted with ponderous brass tongs a few coals and placed them on the smoldering bed in the delicately tinted fireplace. After which she stood before it in the attitude of one who is waiting though not with stolid and undisturbed patience.

A clock ticked loudly on the mantel; she looked at it, around her at the shadows of two beautiful marbles on pedestals of malachite. Moving into the bedroom beyond, she took from a wardrobe of old French workmanship a rose dressing-gown; this, and a pair of slippers of like color she brought out and placed near the fire. As she did so, she started, straightened suddenly; then her expression changed; the voice of Lord Ronsdale without was followed by that of Jocelyn Wray.

"Never fear! They'll get the fellow yet," my lord had said.

Jocelyn answered mechanically; the door opened; the maid caught a glimpse of Ronsdale's face, of the cold eyes that looked the least bit annoyed.

"Although it was most bungling on their part to have permitted him to get away!" he went on. "I hope, however, this little unexpected episode won't disturb your rest." An instant the steely eyes seemed to contemplate her closer. "Many going away to-morrow?" he asked, as if to divert her thoughts from the exciting experience of the evening before leaving her.

"Only Captain Forsythe and--Mr. Steele."

Did he notice the slightest hesitation, on her part, before speaking the last name? My lord's eyes fell; an odd expression appeared on his face. He murmured a few last perfunctory words; then--"They'll get him yet. He can't get away," he repeated. The words had a singular, a sibilant sound; he bowed deferentially and strode off, not toward his own chamber, however, but toward the great stairway leading down to the first story.

As the door closed behind her young mistress, the maid came quickly forward. "Did you learn anything more, Miss Jocelyn, if I may be so bold as to ask, from the police agent? Who the criminal was, or--"

"The police agent only said he was an ex-convict, no ordinary one, who had escaped from London and was making for the sea. They got word he was at the village and followed him there but he managed to elude them and they traced him to Strathorn House park, where he had taken refuge. The police did not acquaint Sir Charles, Lord Ronsdale or any one with their purpose, thinking not to alarm us needlessly beforehand. And--I believe that is all."

A moment the woman waited. "I--shall I--"

The girl looked before her; tiny flames from the grate heightened the sheen on her gown; they threw passing lights on the somewhat tired, proud face. "I shall not need you, Dobson," she said. "You may go. A moment." The woman, who had half-turned, waited; Jocelyn's glance had lowered to the fire; in its reflection her slim, delicate fingers were rosy. She unclasped them, smoothed the brocade absently with one hand. "One or two are leaving early to-morrow. You will see--you will give instructions that everything is provided for their comfort."

The maid responded and left the room; Jocelyn stood as if wrapped in reverie. At length she stirred suddenly and extinguishing all but one dim light, sank back into a chair. Her eyes half closed, then shut entirely. One might have thought her sleeping, except that her breathing was not deep enough; the golden head remained motionless against the soft pink of the dressing-gown; the hand that dropped limply from the white wrist over the arm of the chair did not stir. Around, all was stillness; time passed; then a faint shout from somewhere in the gardens, far off, aroused her. The girl looked around; but immediately silence again reigned; she got up.

Leaning against the shaft holding one of the marbles, she regarded without seeing a chaste, youthful Canova, and beyond, painted on boards and set against satin, a Botticelli face, spiritual, sphinx-like. Her brows were slightly drawn; she breathed deeply now, as if there were something in the place, its quiescence, the immobility of the lovely but ghost-like semblance of faces with which it was peopled that oppressed her. She seemed to be thinking, or questioning herself, when suddenly her attention was attracted again by a sound of a different kind, or was it only fancy? She looked toward a large Flemish tapestry covering one entire end of the room; behind the antique landscape in green threads she knew there was a disused door leading into armory hall. Drawing back the heavy folds she stepped a little behind them; the door was locked and bolted; moreover, several heavy nails had fastened it, completely isolating her suite, as it were, from that spacious, general apartment.

Again the sound! This time she placed it--the creaking of the giant branch of ivy that ran up and around her own balcony. The girl paused irresolutely, her hand on the heavy ancient hanging. Leaning forward she waited; but the noise stopped; she heard nothing more, told herself it was nothing and was about to move out again when her gaze was suddenly held by something that passed like a shadow--a man's arm?--on the other side of the nearest window, between the modern French curtains, not quite drawn together.

In that inconsiderable space between the silk fringes she was sure she had seen it, and anything suggestive of dolce far niente disappeared from the girl's blue eyes. The window opened wider, noiselessly but quickly; then a hand, strong, shapely, pushed the curtains aside. Had the intruder first satisfied himself that the room was vacant? He acted as one certain of his ground; now drawing the window draperies quickly together behind him as if seeking to escape observation from any one below, he stepped out into the room.

Something he saw seemed to surprise him; a low exclamation fell from his lips; his eyes, searching in the dim light his surroundings, swiftly passed from the rich furnishings, the artistic decorations, to the bright-colored robe, the little slippers before the fire. Here they lingered, but only for a moment! Did the intruder hear a sound, a quick breath? His gaze swerved to the opposite end of the room where it saw a living presence. For a moment they looked at each other; the man's face turned very pale; his hand touched the back of a chair; he steadied himself.

"I thought--to enter armory hall--did not know your rooms were here," he managed to say in a low tone, "at this corner of Strathorn House."

She did not answer; so they stood, silently, absurdly. Her face was like paper; her hair, in contrast, most bright; her eyes expressed only incomprehension. The man had to speak first; he pulled himself together. The bad fortune that had dogged him so long, that he had fought against so hard, now found its culmination: it had cast him, of all places, hither, at her feet.

Illustration: I had hoped you would never know Page

I had hoped you would never know Page

So be it; well, destiny now could harm him little more! His eyes gleamed; a reckless light shone out, a daredevil luster. He continued to look at her, then threw back his head.

"I had hoped you would never know; but the gods, it seems," he could even laugh, "have ordained otherwise. 'Fata obstant.'" Still that startled, uncomprehending look on the girl's white face! He went on more quickly, like a man driven to bay. "You do not understand; you are credulous; take people for what they seem,--not for what they are; or have been."

He stopped; a suggestion of pain creeping into her expression, as if, behind wonderment, she was conscious of something being rudely torn, wrenched in her inmost being, held him. His face grew set; the nails of his closed fingers cut his palms. But the laugh returned to his lips, the luster to his eyes.

"Or have been!" he repeated. "A good many people have their pasts. Can you imagine what mine may have been?"

But she scarcely followed his words; she did not think, she could not; she seemed to stand in a hateful dream! Looking at him--the torn evening clothes!--his face, pale, different! Listening to him!--to what--?

"A convict!" said the man. "Yes; that's what I was. Had been in jails, jails! And was sent out of the country, years ago, transported. But time went by and the convict thought he might safely come back--boldly--with impunity. The years and--circumstances had altered him--wrought great changes. He felt compelled to return--why, is of no moment!--believed himself secure in so doing--and was--until chance led him out of his accustomed way--to new walks--new faces--where lay the danger--the ambush, into which he, who thought himself strong, like a weak fool, walked--or was led--blindly." He caught himself up with a laugh. "But what is this to you? Enough, the convict found himself recognized, his identity thoroughly established."

He waited; still she was silent; the little hands clasped tightly the heavy drapery that moved as if she were putting part of her weight on it. Her expression showed still that she had not yet had time to comprehend; that for her what he said remained, even now, but words, confused, inexplicable. A strange sequel to a strange night, a night that had begun with such gaiety and blitheness; that had been interrupted, after he had left her, by the shouting and rough voices from the garden! She seemed to hear them anew, and afterward, the explanation of that odd little person, the police agent, his apologies for breaking in upon the cotillion. But he had said--?

The blue eyes bent like stars now on this man in her room, standing before her with bold, mocking face, as if his dark eyes read, understood every thought that passed through her brain.

"You!--then it was you--John Steele--that they--"

"The convict they tried to arrest? Yes."

"You? I don't--" Her voice was almost childlike.

"I will help you to--understand!" An ashen shade came over his face, but it passed quickly; his voice sounded brusk. "For months, since a fatal evening all light, brilliancy, beauty!--the convict has been trying to hold back the inevitable; but the net whose first meshes were then woven, has since been drawing closer--closer. In the world two forces are ever at work, the pursuers and the pursued. In this instance the former," harshly, "were unusually clever. He struggled hard to keep up the deception until he could complete a defense worthy of the name. But to no avail! He felt the end near; did not expect it so soon, however, this night!--this very night--!"

The man paused; there was a strange gleam in the dark eyes that lingered on her; its light was succeeded by another, a fiercer expression. For the first time she moved, shrank back slightly. "I'm afraid I used a few of them roughly," he said with look derisory. "There was no time for soft talk; it was cut and run--give 'leg bail,' as the thieves say." Did he purposely relapse into coarser words to clench home the whole damning, detestable truth? Her fine soft lips quivered; it may be she felt herself awakening--slowly; one hand pressed now at her breast. In the grate the fire sank, although a few licking flames still thrust their fiery tongues between black lumps of coal.

"But it was a close call, out there in the garden! They were before the convict in the woods; he must needs double back to the shadow of the house! At the bottom of a moat he looked up to a balcony overhead, small as Juliet's--- though I swear he thought it led to armory hall, not here; had he known the truth, he would have stayed there first, and--But, as it was, he heard voices around the corner; afar, men approaching. The ivy at Strathorn House is almost as old as the house itself, the main branches larger than a man's arm. It was not difficult to get here, though I wish now--" he dared smile bitterly--"they had come on me first."

The breeze at the window slightly shook the curtain; it waved in and out; the tassels struck faint taps on the sill.

"But why--?" she began at length, then stopped, as if the question were gone almost as soon as it suggested itself.

"--did I return here,--reenter Strathorn House?" he completed it for her. "Because there seemed nothing else to do; it was probably only temporizing with the inevitable--but one always temporizes."

She moved slowly out into the room; his face was half-averted; all the light that came from the grate, rested now on hers. At that instant she seemed like a shadow, beautiful, but a shadow, going toward him as through no volition of her own. The thick texture on the floor drowned the sound of her steps; she paused with her fingers on the gilded frame of a settee. He did not turn, although he must have known she was near; with his back toward her he gazed down at the soft, bright hues of the rug, and on it a white thing, a tiny bit of lace, a handkerchief that some time before had fluttered to the floor and had been left lying there.

"But--" she spoke now--"you--you who seemed all that was--I can't believe--it is impossible--inconceivable--"

His features twitched, the nerves seemed moving beneath the skin; but he answered in a hard tone. "I have told you the truth; because," the words broke from him, "I had to! Must I," despite himself there was an accent of acutest pain in his voice, "repeat it?"

"No!" said the girl. "Oh, no."

"You guessed I was going away. I was going so that you might never learn what you know now."

"I--guessed you were going? Ah, to-night--on the balcony!"

Did he divine what her words recalled, could not but bring to mind? A tint sprang to her white face; it spread even to the white throat. The blue eyes grew hard, very hard; the little hand he had so short a while before held in his, closed; the slender figure which had then seemed to waver, straightened. He read the thought his words had evoked, did not meet her eyes now.

"You tell me what you have--And yet you have come--dared to come here--under this roof--?"

It may be she also recalled his look when first he had entered this room, and, turning, had seen her; that her mind retained the impress of a bearing, bold, mocking.

"Oh," she said, "it was infamous!"

The word struck him like a whip, lashed his face to a dull red; the silence grew.

"I would not presume to dispute or to contradict any conclusion you may have reached," he spoke at length in a low, even voice. "I had not, as I said, intended this last, this most inexcusable intrusion. You have now only one course to pursue--" His gaze turned to the long silken bell-rope on the wall. "And I promise not to resist."

Her glance followed his, returned to his face, to his eyes, quietly challenging. She took a step.

"Well?" he said.

She had suddenly stopped; in the hall voices were heard approaching; he too caught them.

"That simplifies matters," he remarked.

Her breast stirred; she stood listening; they came nearer--now were at the door. A measured knocking broke the stillness.

"Jocelyn!" The voice was that of Sir Charles. "Are you there?" She did not answer. "Kindly unlock the door."

CHAPTER XIV

AN ANSWER

The girl made no motion to obey and the knocking was repeated; mechanically she moved toward the threshold. "Yes?" All the color had left her face. "What--what is it?"

"Don't mean to alarm you, my dear, but Mr. Gillett thinks the convict might be concealing himself somewhere in the house; indeed, that it is quite likely. So we are making a little tour of inspection. Shall we not go through your rooms? There! don't be frightened!" quickly, "only as a matter of precaution, you know."

"I," she seemed to catch her breath, "it is really quite unnecessary. I have been through them myself."

"Might have known that!" with an attempt at jocoseness. "But thought we would make sure. Your balcony, you have looked there?"

"Yes."

"Very well; lock your window leading to it. Only as a matter of precaution," he repeated hastily. "No need of our coming in, I fancy. You had retired?"

"I--was about to."

"Quite right." A moment the party lingered. "Shall I send one of the maids to sleep in your dressing-room? Company, you know! Your voice sounds a little nervous."

"Does it? Not at all!" she said hastily. "I am--not in the least nervous."

"Good night, then!" They went. "One of my men in the garden felt sure he had seen him return toward the house," Mr. Gillett's voice was wafted back, became fainter, died away.

The man in the room stood motionless now, his face like that of a statue save for the light and life of his eyes. The clock beat the moments; he looked at her. The girl was almost turned from him; he saw more of the bright hair than the pale profile, so still against the delicately carved arabesques of the panel.

"The other way would have been--preferable!"

There was nothing reckless or bold in his bearing now; but, looking away, she did not see. Was he tempted, if only in an infinitesimal degree, to suggest a plea of mitigating circumstances--not for his own sake but for hers; that she might feel less keenly that sense of hurt, of outraged pride, for having smiled on him, admitted him to a certain frank, free intimacy? Before the words fell from his lips, however, she turned; her gaze arrested his purpose, made him feel poignantly, acutely, the distance now between them. "What were you," she hesitated, emphasized over-sharply the word, "transported for?"

An instant his eyes flashed suddenly back at her, as if he were on the point of answering, telling her all, disavowing; but to what end? To ask more of her than of others, throw himself on her generosity?

"What does it matter?"

True; what did it matter to her; he had been in prisons before, by his own words.

"Your name, of course, is not John Steele?"

He confessed it a purloined asset.

"What was it?"

He looked at her--beyond! To a storm-tossed ship, a golden-haired child, her curls in disorder, moving with difficulty, yet clinging so steadfastly to a small cage. His name? It may be he heard again the loud pounding and knocking; held her once more to his breast, felt the confiding, soft arms.

"What does it matter?" he repeated.

What, indeed? That which she had not been able to penetrate, to understand in him, this was it! This!

"But why"--fragments of what he had said recurred to her; she spoke mechanically--"when you found yourself recognized, did you not leave England; why did you come here--to Strathorn House; incur the danger, the risk?"

"Why?" He still continued to look straight before him. "Because you--were here!" IIe spokc quietly, simply.

"I?" she trembled.

"Oh, you need not fear!" quickly. "You!" a bitter smile crossed his face. "One may see a star and long to draw nearer it, though one knows it is always beyond reach, unattainable! May even stumble forward, led by its light-- bright, beautiful! Whither?" He laughed abruptly. "One has not asked, nor cared."

"Cared?" Her figure swayed; he too stood uncertainly; the lights seemed to tremble.

The man suddenly straightened; then turned. "And now," his voice sounded harsh, tense; he stepped toward the balcony.

His words, the abrupt action--what it portended, aroused her.

"No; no!" The exclamation broke from her involuntarily; she seemed to waken as from something unreal that had momentarily held her. "There-- there may be a safer way!" She hardly knew what she was saying; one thought alone possessed her mind; she looked with strained, bright glance before her. "The Queen Elizabeth staircase leading into the garden from my-- " The words were arrested; her blue eyes, dark, dilated, lingered on him in an odd, impersonal way. "Wait!" Bright spots of color now tinted her cheeks; she went quickly toward the door she had left, her manner that of one who hastens to some course on impulse, without pausing to reason. "A few minutes!" She listened, turned the key; then opening the door, stepped hastily out into the hall.

The latch clicked; the man stood alone. Whatever her purpose, only the desire to act quickly, to have done with an intolerable situation moved him. Once more he looked toward the window through which he had entered; first, however, before going, he bethought himself of something, an answer to one of her questions. She should find the answer after he was gone! His fingers thrust themselves into a breast-pocket; he took out a small object, wrapped in velvet. An instant his eyes rested upon it; then, stooping, he picked up the bit of lace handkerchief from the floor and laying the dark velvet against it placed the two on the table.

Would she understand? The debt he had felt he owed her long before to-night, that sense of obligation to the child who had reached out her hand, in a different life, a different world! No; she had, of course, forgotten; still he would leave it, that talisman so precious, which he had cherished almost superstitiously.

When a few minutes later the girl hastily reëntered the room, she carried on her arm a man's coat and hat; her appearance was feverish, her eyes wide and shining.

"Your clothes are torn--would attract attention! These were on the rack--I don't know whose--but I stole them!--stole them!"

She spoke quickly with a little hard note of self-mockery. Her voice broke off suddenly; she looked around her.

The coat and hat slipped from her arm; she looked at the window; the curtain still moved, as if a hand had but recently touched it. She stared at it--incredulously. He had gone; he would have none of her assistance then; preferred--She listened, but caught only the rustling of the heavy silk. When? Minutes passed; at her left, a candle, carelessly adjusted by the maid, dripped to the dresser; its over-long wick threw weird, ever-changing shadows; her own silhouette appeared in various distorted forms on hangings and wall.

Still she heard nothing, nothing louder than the faint sounds at the window; the occasional, mysterious creakings of old woodwork. He must have long since reached the ground--the bottom of the old moat; perhaps, as the police agent and several of his men were in the house, he might even have attained the fringe of the wood. It was not so far distant,--the space intervening from the top of the moat contained many shrubs; in their friendly shadows--

She stole to the corner of the window now and cautiously peered out. The sky was overcast; below, faint markings could just be discerned; beyond, Cimmerian gloom--Strathorn wood.

Had he reached, could he reach it? A cool breeze fanned her cheeks without lessening the flush that burned there; her lips were half-parted. She stepped uncertainly back; a reaction swept over her; the most trivial thoughts came to mind. She remembered that she had not locked the door of her boudoir; that Sir Charles had told her to do so. She almost started to obey; but laughed nervously instead. How absurd! What, however, should she do? She looked toward the next room. Go to bed? It seemed the commonplace, natural conclusion, and, after all, life was very commonplace. But the coat and hat she had brought there? Consideration of them, also, came within the scope of the commonplace.

It did not take her long to dispose of them, not on the rack, however. Standing again, a few moments later, at the head of the stairway, in the upper hall, she heard voices approaching. Whereupon she quickly dropped both hat and coat on a chair near-by and fled to her room.

None too soon! From above footsteps were descending; people now passed by; they evidently had been searching the third story. She could hear their low, dissatisfied voices; the last persons to come she at once recognized by their tones.

"You have made a bungling job of it," said Lord Ronsdale. There was a suppressed fierce bitterness in his accents, which, however, in the excitement of the moment, the girl failed to notice.

"He had made up his mind not to be taken alive, my Lord."

"Then--" The other interrupted Mr. Gillett harshly, but she failed to catch more of his words.

"We've not lost him, my Lord," Mr. Gillett spoke again. "If he's not in the house, he's near it, in the garden, and we have every way guarded."

"Every way guarded!" The girl drew her breath; as they disappeared, the striking of the clock caused her to start. One! two! About four hours of darkness, hardly that long remained for him! And yet she would have supposed it later; it had been after one o'clock when she had come to her room.

She became aware of a throbbing in her head, a dull pain, and mechanically seating herself near one of the tables, she put up her hand and started to draw the pins from her hair, but soon desisted. Again she began to think, more clearly this time, more poignantly, of all she had experienced--listened to--that night!

She, a Wray, sprung from a long line of proud, illustrious folk! And he? The breath of the roses outside was wafted upward; her eyes, deep, self-scoffing, rested, without seeing, on a small dark object on a handkerchief on the table. What was it to her if they took him?--What indeed? Her fingers played with the object, closed hard on it. Why should she care if he paid the penalty; he, a self-confessed---

Something fell from the velvet covering in her hand and struck with a musical sound on the hard, polished top. Amid a turmoil of thoughts, she was vaguely aware of it gleaming there on the cold white marble, a small disk--a gold coin. At first it seemed only to catch without interesting her glance; then slowly she took it, as if asking herself how it came there, on her handkerchief, which, she dimly remembered, had been lying on the floor. Some one, of course, must have picked up the handkerchief; but no one had been in the room since she had noticed it except--

Her gaze swung to the window; he, then, had left it. Why? What had she to do with anything that had been his?

More closely she scrutinized it, the shining disk on her rosy palm; a King George gold piece! Above the monarch's face and head with its flowing locks, appeared a tiny hole, as if some one had once worn it; beneath, just discernible, was the date, . She continued to regard it; then looked again at the bit of velvet, near-by. It had been wrapped in that, carefully; for what reason? Like something more than what it seemed--a mere gold piece!

"." Why, even as she gazed at the cloth, felt it, did the figures seem to reiterate themselves in her brain? "." There could be nothing especially significant about the date; yet even as she concluded thus, by some introspective process she saw herself bending over, studying those figures on another occasion. Herself--and yet--

She was looking straight before her now; suddenly she started and sprang up. "A King George gold piece!" Her hair, unbound, fell around her, below her waist; her eyes like sapphires, gazed out from a veritable shimmer of gold. "Date--" She paused. "Why, this belonged to me once, as a child, and I--"

The blue eyes seemed searching--searching; abruptly she found what she sought. "I gave it to the convict on the Lord Nelson." She almost whispered the words. "The brave, brave fellow who sacrificed his life for mine." Her warm fingers closed softly on the coin; she seemed wrapped in the picture thus recalled.

"Then how--" Her brows knitted, she swept the shining hair from her face. "If he were drowned, how could it have been left here by--" Her eyes were dark now with excitement. "Him? Him?" she repeated. "Unless," her breast suddenly heaved--"he was not drowned, after all; he--"

A sudden shot from the park rang out; the coin fell from the girl's hand; other shots followed. She ran out upon the balcony, a stifled cry on her lips; she stared off, but only the darkness met her gaze.

CHAPTER XV

CURRENTS AND COUNTER CURRENTS

Not far from one of the entrances to Regent's Park or the hum of Camden Town's main artery of traffic, lay a little winding street which, because of its curving lines, had long been known as Spiral Row. Although many would not deign in passing to glance twice down this modest thoroughfare, it presented, nevertheless, a romantic air of charm and mystery. The houses nestled timidly behind time-worn walls; it was always very quiet within this limited precinct, and one wondered sometimes, by day, if the various secluded abodes were really inhabited, and by whom? An actress, said vague rumor; a few scribblers, a pair of painters, a military man or two. Here Madam Grundy never ventured, but Calliope and the tuneful nine were understood to be occasional callers. One who once lived in the Row has likened it to a tiny Utopia where each and every one minded his own business and where the comings and goings of one's neighbor were matters of indifference.

Into this delectable byway there turned, late in the night of the second day after that memorable evening at Strathorn House, a man who, looking quickly around him, paused before the closed gate of one of the dwellings. The street, ever a quiet one, appeared at that advanced hour absolutely deserted, and, after a moment's hesitation, the man pulled the bell; for some time he waited; but no response came. He looked in; through the shrubbery he could dimly make out the house, set well back, and in a half uncertain way he stood staring at it, when from the end of the street, he heard a vehicle coming rapidly toward him.

More firmly the man jerked at the handle of the bell; this time his efforts were successful; a glimmer as from a candle appeared at the front door, and a few minutes later a dark form came slowly down the graveled walk. As it approached the vehicle also drew nearer; the man regarded the latter sidewise; now it was opposite him, and he turned his back quickly to the flare of its lamps. But in a moment it had whirled by, with a note of laughter from its occupants, light pleasure seekers; at the same time a key turned in a lock and the gate swung open.

"Good evening, Dennis," said the caller. The faint gleam of the candle revealed the drowsy and unmistakably Celtic face of him he addressed, a man past middle age, who regarded the new-comer with a look of recognition. "I'm afraid I've interrupted your slumbers. This is rather a late hour at which to arrive."

"No matter, sir. Sure and I sat up expecting you, Mr. Steele, until after midnight, and had only just turned in when--"

"What--?" The new-comer, now fairly within the garden, could not suppress a start of surprise, which however the other, engaged in relocking the gate, did not appear to notice. "Expecting--?"

"Although I'd given up thinking you'd be here to-night," the latter went on. "But won't you be stepping in, sir?"

The other silently followed, walking in the manner of one tired and worn; he did not, however, at that moment seem concerned with fatigue or physical discomfort; the uncertain light of the candle before him showed his brows drawn, his eyes questioning, as if something had happened to cause him to think deeply, doubtfully. At the door the servant stood aside to allow him to enter; then ushered him into a fairly commodious and comfortable sitting-room.

"My master did not come back with you, sir, from Strathorn House?"

"No; Captain Forsythe's gone on to Germany."

"To attend some court, I suppose. Sure, 'tis a dale he has done of that, Mr. Steele, after the both of us were wounded by those black devils in India and retired from active service." The servant's voice had an inquiring accent; his glance rested now in some surprise on the new-comer's garments,--a gamekeeper's well-worn coat and cap,--and on the dusty, almost shabby-looking shoes.

"A wager," said John Steele, noting the old orderly's expression. "From Strathorn House to London by foot, within a given time, don't you know; fell in with some rough customers last night who thought my coat and hat better than these."

"I beg your pardon, sir, but--" The man's apprehensive look fastened itself on a dark stain on the coat, near the shoulder.

"Just winged me--a scratch," replied John Steele with an indifferent shrug, sinking into a chair near the fire which burned low.

"It's lucky you came off no worse, sir, and you'll be finding a change of garments up-stairs; I put them out for you myself--"

"I'm afraid, Dennis, I'm rather large for your master's clothes," was the visitor's reply in a voice that he strove vainly to make light.

"Sure, they're your own, sir." The other looked up quickly. "I'll get everything ready for a bath, and if you've a mind for anything to eat afterward--"

"I think I'll have a little of the last, first," said the visitor slowly.

"Right you are, sir. You do look a bit done up, sir," sympathetically, "but there's a veal and 'ammer in the cupboard that will soon make you fit."

"One moment, Dennis." John Steele leaned back; the dying embers revealed a haggard face; his eyes half closed as if from lack of sleep but immediately opened again. "You spoke of expecting me; how," he stretched out his legs, "did you know--?"

"Sure, sir, by your luggage; it arrived with my master's heavier boxes that he didn't take along with him over the wather." The listener did not stir; was he too weary to experience surprise or even deeper emotion?

His luggage there!--where no one knew--could have known, he was going! The place he had selected, under what he had considered propitious circumstances, as a haven, a refuge; where he might find himself for a brief period comparatively safe, could he reach it, turn in, without being detected! This last he believed he had successfully accomplished; and then to be told by the man--All John Steele's excuses for coming in this unceremonious fashion that he had planned to put to the servant of Captain Forsythe were at the moment forgotten. Who could have guessed that he would make his way straight hither--or had any one? An enemy, divining a lurking place for which he was heading, would not have obligingly forwarded his belongings. What then? Had Jocelyn Wray ordered them sent on with Captain Forsythe's boxes and bags, in order that they might be less likely to fall into the hands of the police?

This line of reasoning seemed to lead into most unwonted channels; it was not probable she would concern herself so much further about a common fugitive. The cut and bruised fingers of the man before the fireplace linked and unlinked; an indefinable feeling of new dangers he had not calculated on assailed him. Suppose the police should have learned--should elect to trace, those articles of his? It was a contingency, a hazard to be considered; he knew that every possible effort would be made to find him; that if his antagonists were eager before, they would embark on the present quest with redoubled zeal. He had been in their hands and had got away; disappointment would drive them more fiercely on to employ every expedient. They might even now be at the gate; at the moment, however, he felt as if he hardly cared, only that he was very tired, too exhausted to move on. His exertions of the last few days had been of no ordinary kind; his shoulder was stiff and it pained.

"Here you are, sir." The servant had entered and reëntered, had set the table without the man in the arm-chair being conscious of his coming and going. "Remembered my master inviting you once, when you were here, to pitch your camp at Rosemary Villa any time you should be after yearning for that quietood essential for literary composition and to windin' up the campaign on your book. So when I saw your luggage--"

"Exactly." It was curious the man should have spoken thus, should have voiced one of the very subterfuges Steele had had in mind himself to utter, to show pretext for his too abrupt appearance. But now--?

The situation was changed; yet he felt too exhausted to disavow the servant's conclusion. Certainly the episode of the luggage had made his task easier at this point; only, however, to enhance the greater hazards, as if fate were again laughing at him, offering him too much ease, too great comfort, seeking to allure him with a false estimate of his security. As he ate, mechanically, but with the zest of one who had long fasted, he listened; again a vehicle went by; then another.

"Rather livelier than usual to-night?" he observed and received an affirmative answer. Some evenings now you'd hardly ever hear anything passing from sunset to sunrise and find it as quiet as the tomb.

Who lived on the right, on the left? The visitor asked several questions casually; the house to the right, the man thought, might be vacant; no one appeared to live in it very long. At least the moving van seemed to have acquired a habit of stopping there; the one on the left had a more stable tenant; a lady who appeared in the pantomime, or the opera, he wasn't sure which,--only, foreign people sometimes went in and out.

John Steele rose with an effort; no, there was nothing more he required, except rest! Which room would he prefer, he was asked when he found himself on the upper landing; the man had put his things in a front chamber; but the back one was larger. John Steele forced himself to consider; he even inspected both of the rooms; that on the front floor had one window facing the Row; the second chamber looked out over a rear wall separating the vegetable garden of Rosemary Villa from the shrub-adorned confines of a place which fronted on the next street.

The visitor decided on the former chamber; he carefully closed the blinds and drew across the window the dark, heavy curtains. This would answer very well; excellent accommodations for a man whose own chambers in the city were now in the hands of renovators--the painters, the paper-hangers, the plumbers. And the back room? He paused, as if considering the servant's assumption of his purpose in coming hither. He might as well let the fellow think--

Yes, he would venture to make use of that for his work; could thus take advantage of the force of circumstances that had arisen to alienate him from prosaic citations, writs or arraignments. But he must, with strained lightness, emphasize one point; for a brief spell he did not wish to be disturbed. People might call; people probably would, anxious clients, almost impossible to get rid of, unless--

No one must know where he was, under any circumstances; his voice sounded almost jocular, at singular variance with the heaviness, the weariness of his face. He, the old servant, had been a soldier; knew how to fulfil, then, a request or an order. Something crinkled in the speaker's hand, passed to the other who was now busying himself with the bath; the man's moist fingers did not hesitate to close on the note. He had been a hardened campaigner and incidentally a good forager; he remarked at once he would carry out to the letter all his master's visitor asked.

Half an hour later, John Steele, clad in his dressing-gown, sat alone near the fire in his room; every sound had ceased save at intervals a low creaking of old timber. Now it came from overhead, then from the hall or near the window, as if spirit feet or fingers were busy in that venerable, quaint domicile. But these faint noises, inseparable from houses with a history, John Steele did not hear; the food and the bath had awakened in him a momentary alertness; he seemed waiting--for what? Something that did not happen; heaviness, depression again weighed on him; to keep awake he stirred himself and again glanced about. Here were evidences of odd taste on the part of the tenant in the matter of household decoration; a chain and ball that had once been worn by a certain famous convict reposed on an étagère, instead of the customary vase or jug of pottery; other souvenirs of prisons and the people that had been in them adorned a few shelves and brackets.

John Steele smiled grimly; but soon his thoughts seemed floating off beyond control, and rising suddenly, he threw himself on the bed. For a moment he strove to consider one or two tasks that should have been accomplished this night but which he must defer; was vaguely conscious of the slamming of a blind next door; then over-strained nature yielded.

Hours passed; the sun rose high in the heavens, began to sink; still the heavy sleep of utter exhaustion claimed him. Once or twice the servant came to the door, listened, and stole away again. The afternoon was well advanced when, as half through a dream, John Steele heard the rude jingling of a bell,--the catmeat man, or the milkman, drowsily he told himself. In fancy he seemed to see the broad, flowing river from a window of his own chambers, the dawn stealing over, marshaling its tints,--crimson until--

Slowly through the torpor of his brain realization began also to dawn; this room?--it was not his. The gleaming lances of sunlight that darted through the half-closed shutters played on the strange wall-paper of a strange apartment; no, he remembered it now--last night!

The loud and emphatic closing of the front gate served yet more speedily to arouse him; hastily he sat up; his head buzzed from a long-needed sleep that had been over sound; his limbs still ached, but every sense on an instant became unnaturally keen. Footsteps resounded on the gravel; he heard voices; those of two men, who were coming toward the house.

"So it's the meter man you are?" John Steele recognized the inquiring voice as that of the caretaker. "Sure, you're a new one from the last that was here."

"Yes; we change beats occasionally," was the careless answer, as the men passed around the side of the house and entered a rear door. For a time there was silence; John Steele sprang from his bed and crept very softly toward the hall. "A new man--" He heard them talking again after a few minutes; he remained listening at his door, now slightly ajar.

"There must be a leak somewhere from the quantity you've burned. I'll have a look around; might save your master a few shillings."

The man moved from room to room and started, at length, up the stairs. John Steele closed and noiselessly locked his door; the "meter man" crossed the upper hall and stepped, one after the other, into the several rooms. Having apparently made there the necessary examination, he walked over and tried the door of John Steele's room.

"This room's occupied by a visitor," interposed the servant quickly in a hushed voice. "And he's asleep now; he wouldn't thank you for the disturbing of his repose."

"All right." Did the listener detect an accent of covert satisfaction in the caller's low tones? "I'll not wake him. Don't find the leak I was looking for; will drop in again, though, when I have more time."

Their footsteps receded and shortly afterward, the man left the house; as he did so, John Steele, pushing back the blinds a little, looked out of his room; the man who had reached the front of the place glanced back. His gaze at that instant, meeting the other's, seemed to betray a momentary eagerness; quickly Steele turned away; no doubt now lingered in his mind as to the purpose of the visit.

CHAPTER XVI

FLIGHT

The half-expected had happened; bag and baggage had led his pursuers hither; the fellow could now go back and report. After his bath, before lying down, John Steele had partly dressed in the garments laid out for him; now he threw the dressing-gown from his shoulders and hastily put on the rest of his clothes. He felt now only the need for action--to do what? Impatience was capped by the realization of his own impotence; Rosemary Villa was, no doubt, at that very moment, subjected to a close espionage. He heard the man-servant in the garden, and unable to restrain a growing restlessness to know the worst, Steele mounted the stairs to the attic.

From the high window there he could see, around a curve in the Row, a loitering figure; in the other direction a neighboring house concealed the byway, but he could reasonably conclude that some one also sauntered there, sentinel at that end of the street. Quickly coming down to the second story, he began cautiously to examine from the windows the situation of the house, in relation to adjoining grounds and neighboring dwellings.

To the right, the top of the high wall shone with the customary broken bits of glass; the rear defenses glistened also in formidable fashion. He noted, however, several places where this safeguard against unwonted invasion showed signs of deterioration; in one or two spots the jagged fragments had been broken, or had fallen off. These slight breaks in the continuity of irregular, menacing glass bits, he fixed in mind by a certain shrub or tree. Against the rear wall, which was of considerable height, leaned his neighbor's low conservatory, almost spanning it from side to side.

"Sure, sir, I don't know whether it's breakfast or supper that's waiting for you." Captain Forsythe's man had reappeared and stood now at the top of the landing looking in at him. "It's a sound sleep you've had."

John Steele glanced at the clock; the afternoon was waning. Why did not his enemies force their way in, surround him at once? Unless--and this might prove a momentary saving clause!--these people without were but an advance guard, an outpost, awaiting orders. In this event Gillett would hastily be sent for; would soon be on his way---

"'Tis a rasher of real Irish bacon that is awaiting your convenience, sir."

The servant was now eying the visitor dubiously; John Steele wheeled, a perfunctory answer on his lips, and going to the dining-room swallowed hastily a few mouthfuls. From where he sat he could command a view of the front gate, and kept glancing toward it when alone. To go now,--or wait? The daylight did not favor the former course unless his pursuers should suddenly appear before the locked gate, demanding admission.

He made up his mind as to his course then, the last desperate shift. Amid a turmoil of thoughts a certain letter he had had in mind to send to Captain Forsythe occurred to him, and calling for paper and pen, he wrote there, facing the window, feverishly, hastily, several pages; then he gave the letter to the servant for the postman, whose special call at the iron knocker without had just sounded. The letter would have served John Steele ill had it fallen into his enemies' hands, but once in the care of the royal mails it would be safe. If it were, indeed, that person at the gate, and not some one--

"One moment, Dennis!" The man paused. "Of course you will make sure it is the postman--?"

The servant stared at this guest whose demeanor was becoming more and more eccentric. "As if I didn't know his knock!" he said, departing.

The afternoon waned; the shadows began to fall; John Steele's pulses now throbbed expectantly. He called for a key to the gate and moved toward the front door; by this time the darkness had deepened, and, key in hand, he stepped out.

At first he walked toward the front on the gravel that the servant might hear him, but near the entrance he paused, hesitating, to look out. As he remained thus, some one, who had been standing not far off, drew near. This person steathily passed; in doing so he glanced around; but John Steele felt uncertain whether the fellow had or had not been able to distinguish him in the gloom. John Steele waited, however, until the other moved a short distance on; then he retraced his own way quietly, keeping to the grass, toward the house; near it he swerved and in the same rapid manner stole around the place until he reached the back wall.

There he examined his position, felt the top, then placed his fingers on the wall. It was about six feet high, but seizing hold, he was about to spring into the air, when behind him, from the direction of the Row, a low metallic sound caught his attention. The front gate to the Forsythe house had suddenly clicked; some one had entered,--not the servant; John Steele had seen him but a few moments before in the kitchen; some one, then, who had quietly picked the lock, as the surest way of getting in.

John Steele looked back; even as he did so, a number of figures abruptly ran forward from the gate. He waited no longer but drew himself up to a level with the top of the wall. The effort made him acutely aware of his

wounded shoulder; he winced but set his teeth hard and swung himself over
until one foot came in contact with the iron frame of the greenhouse next to
the masonry. To crawl to the end of the lean-to, bending to hold to the wall,
and then to let himself down, occupied but a brief interval.

As he stood there, trying to make out a path through shrubs and trees, he
heard behind him an imperative knocking at the front door of Captain
Forsythe's house; the expostulating tones of the serving-man; the half-
indistinct replies that were succeeded by the noise of feet hastening into the
house.

For some time nothing save these sounds was wafted to the listener; then a
loud disappointed voice, sounding above another voice, came from a half-
opened window. John Steele stood still no longer; great hazard, almost
certain capture, lay before him in the direction he was going; the street this
garden led to would be watched; but he could not remain where he was.
Already his enemies were moving about in the neighboring grounds; soon
they would flash their lights over the wall, would discover him, unless--He
moved quickly forward. As he neared the house, more imposing than
Captain Forsythe's, a stream of light poured from a window; through this
bright space he darted quickly, catching a fleeting view of people within,
several with their faces turned toward him. Close to a side of the square-
looking house, he paused, his heart beating fast--not with fear, but with a
sudden, fierce anger at the possibility that he would be caught thus; no
better than a mere--

But needs must, when the devil drives; the devil was driving him now hard.
To attempt to reach the gate, to get out to Surrey Road,--little doubt existed
as to what awaited him there; so, crouching low, he forced himself to linger
a little longer where he was. As thus he remained motionless, sharp twinges
again shot through his shoulder; then, on a sudden, he became unmindful
of physical discomfort; a plan of action that had flashed through his brain,
held him oblivious to all else; it offered only the remotest chance of escape--
but still a chance, which he weighed, determined to take! It had come to him
while listening to the merry voices within the room near him talking of the
gay dinner just ended, of the box party at the theater that was to follow.

Already cabs were at the door; the women and the men, several of the latter
flushed with wine, were ready to go. A servant walked out and unlocked the
gate and with light badinage the company issued forth. As they did so, John
Steele, unobserved, stepped forward; in the semi-darkness the party passed
through the entrance into the street. Taking his place among the last of the
laughing, dimly-seen figures, John Steele walked boldly on and found
himself a moment later on the sidewalk of Surrey Road. He was aware that

some one, a woman, had touched his arm, as if to take it; of a light feminine voice and an abrupt exclamation of surprise, of the quick drawing back of fluttering skirts. But he did not stop to apologize or to explain; walking swiftly to one of the last cabs he sprang in.

"A little errand first, driver," he called out. "To--" and mentioned a street--"as fast as you can." His tone was sharp, authoritative; it implied the need for instant obedience, rang like a command. The man straightened, touched his horse with his whip, and wheeling quickly they dashed away.

As they did so, John Steele thought he heard exclamations behind; looking through the cab window he saw, at the gate, the company gazing after him, obviously not yet recovered from their thrill of surprise following his unexpected action. He observed, also, two men on the other side of the street who now ran across and held a brief altercation with one of the cabmen. As they were about to enter the cab several persons in the party apparently intervened, expostulating vigorously. It was not difficult to surmise the resentment of the group at this attempted summary seizure of a second one of their cabs. By the time the men had explained their imperative need, and after further argument were permitted to drive off, John Steele had gained a better start than he had dared to hope. But they would soon be after him, post-haste; yes, already they were dashing hard and furiously behind; he lifted the lid overhead, in his hand a sovereign.

"Those men must not overtake us, cabby. Go where you will! You understand?"

The man did; his fingers closed quickly on the generous tip and once more he lashed his horse. For some time they continued at a rapid pace, now skirting the confines of the park, now plunging into a puzzling tangle of streets; but wherever they went, the other cab managed always to keep them in sight. It even began to creep up, nearer. From his pocket John Steele drew a weapon; his eyes gleamed ominously. The pursuing hansom drew closer; casting a hurried glance over his shoulder, he again called up to the driver.

"It's no use, gov'ner," came back the reply. "This 'oss 'as been out longer than 'is."

"Then turn the first dark corner and slow up a bit,--for only a second; afterward, go on your very best as long as you can."

Another sovereign changed hands and shortly afterward the vehicle dashed into a side street. It appeared as likely a place as any for his purpose; John Steele, hardly waiting for the man to draw rein, leaped out as far as he might. He landed without mishap, heard a whip snap furiously, and darted back into a doorway. He had just reached it when the other cab drew near; for an instant he felt certain that he had been seen; but the pursuers' eyes were bent eagerly ahead.

"This'll mean a fiver for you, my man," he heard one of them shout to the driver. "We've got him, by--" A harsh, jubilant cry cut the air; then they were gone.

John Steele did not wait; replacing the weapon in his pocket he started quickly around the corner; his cabman could not lead them far; they would soon return. As fast as possible, without attracting undue attention, he retraced his way; passed in and out of tortuous thoroughfares; by shops from whence came the smell of frying fish; down alleys where squalor lurked. Although he had by this time, perhaps, eluded the occupants of the cab, he knew there were others keenly alert for his capture whom he might at any moment encounter. To his fancy every corner teemed with peril; he did not underestimate the resources of those who sought him or the cunning of him who was the chief among his enemies.

Which way should he move? At that moment the city's multitudinous blocks seemed like the many squares of an oriental checker-board; the problem he put to himself was how to cross the city and reach the vicinity of the river; there to make a final effort to look for--What? A hopeless quest!

His face burned with fever; he did not heed it. A long, broad thoroughfare, as he walked on, had suddenly unfolded itself to his gaze; one side of this highway shone resplendent with the flaring lights of numerous stands and stalls displaying vegetables and miscellaneous articles. A hubbub assailed the ear, the voices of hucksters and hawkers, vying with one another to dispose of their wares; like ants, people thronged the sidewalk and pavement near these temporary booths.

About to turn back from this animated scene, John Steele hesitated; the road ran straight and sure toward the destination he wished to reach, while on either hand lay a network of devious ways. Amid these labyrinths, even one familiar with the city's maze might go astray, and again he glanced down the single main road, cutting squarely through all intricacies; noted that although, on one side, the lamps and the torches flared high, revealing every detail of merchandise, and, incidentally, the faces of all who passed, the other side of the thoroughfare seemed the more murky and shadowy by comparison.

He decided, crossed the street; lights gleamed in his face. He pushed his way through the people unmolested and strode on, followed only by the noise of passing vehicles and carts; then found himself walking on the other side, apart from the headlong busy stream. A suspicion of mist hung over the city; through it, people afar assumed shapes unreal; above the jagged sky-line of housetops the heavens had taken on that sickly hue, the high dome's jaundiced aspect for London in autumn.

On!--on! John Steele moved; on!--on!--the traffic pounded, for the most part in the opposite direction; a vast, never-ending source of sound, it seemed to soothe momentarily his sense of insecurity. Time passed; he had, apparently, evaded his pursuers; he told himself he might, after all, meet the problem confronting him; meet and conquer. It would be a hard battle; but once in that part of the city he was striving to reach, he might find those willing to offer him shelter--low-born, miserable wretches he had helped. He would not disdain their succor; the end justified the way. In their midst, if anywhere in London, was the one man in the world who could throw a true light on the events of the past; enable him to---

Behind him some one followed; some one who drew ever nearer, with soft, skulking steps which now he heard--

"Mr. Steele!" Even as he wheeled, his name was called out.

CHAPTER XVII

THE UNEXPECTED

Before the sudden fierce passion gleaming on John Steele's face, the bright flame of his look, the person who had accosted him shrank back; his pinched and pale face showed surprise, fear; almost incoherently he began to stammer. Steele's arm had half raised; it now fell to his side; his eyes continued to study, with swift, piercing glance, the man who had called. He was not a fear-inspiring object; hunger and privation seemed so to have gripped him that now he presented but a pitiable shadow of himself.

Did John Steele notice that changed, abject aspect, that bearing, devoid totally of confidence? All pretense of a certain coster smartness that he remembered, had vanished; the hair, once curled with cheap jauntiness, hung now straight and straggling; a tawdry ornament which had stood out in the past, absurdly distinct on a bright cravat, with many other details that had served to build up a definite type of individual, seemed to have dropped off into oblivion.

Steele looked about; they two, as far as he could see, were alone. He regarded the man again; it was very strange, as if a circular stage, the buskined world's tragic-comic wheel of fortune, had turned, and a person whom he had seen in one character had reappeared in another.

"I ask your pardon." The fellow found his voice. "I'll not be troubling you further, Mr. Steele."

The other's expression altered; he could have laughed; he had been prepared for almost anything, but not this. The man's tones were hopeless; very deferential, however.

"You were about to beg--of me?" John Steele smiled, as if, despite his own danger, despite his physical pangs, he found the scene odd, unexampled, between this man and himself--this man, a sorry vagrant; himself, become now but a--"You were about to--?"

"I had, sir, so far forgotten myself as to venture to think of applying for temporary assistance; however--" Dandy Joe began to shuffle off in a spiritless way, when--

"You are hungry?" said John Steele.

"A little, sir."

"A modest answer in view of the actual truth, I suspect," observed the other. But although his words were brusk, he felt in his pocket; a sovereign--it was all he had left about him. When he had departed post-haste for Strathorn House, he had neglected to furnish himself with funds for an indefinite period; a contingency he should have foreseen had risen; for the present he could not appear at the bank to draw against the balance he always maintained there. His own future, how he should be able to subsist, even if he could evade those who sought him, had thus become problematical. John Steele fingered that last sovereign; started to turn, when he caught the look in the other's eyes. Did it recall to him his own plight but a short twenty-four hours before?

"Very well!" he said, and was about to give the coin to the man and walk away, when another thought held him.

This fellow had been a link in a certain chain of events; the temptation grew to linger with him, the single, tangible, though paltry and useless, figure in the drama he could lay hands on. John Steele looked around; in a byway he saw the lighted window of a cheap oyster buffet. It appeared a place where they were not likely to be interrupted, and motioning to the man, he wheeled abruptly and started for it.

A few minutes later found them seated in the shabby back room; a number of faded sporting pictures adorned the wall; one--how John Steele started!--showed the 'Frisco Pet in a favorite attitude. Absorbed in studying it, he hardly heard the proprietor of the place, and it was Joe who first answered him; he had the honor of being asked there by this gentleman, and--he regarded John Steele expectantly.

Steele spoke now; his dark eyes shone strangely; a sardonic expression lurked there. The proprietor could bring his companion a steak, if he had one. Large or small?--large--with an enigmatical smile.

The "hexibition styke" in the window; would that do, queried the proprietor, displaying it.

Would it? the eyes of the erstwhile dandy of the east side asked of John Steele; that gentleman only answered with a nod, and the supplemental information that he would take "half a dozen natives himself." The proprietor bustled out; from an opposite corner of the room, the only other occupant regarded with casual curiosity the two ill-assorted figures. Tall, florid, Amazonian, this third person represented a fair example of the London grisette, the petite dame who is not very petite, of its thoroughfares. Setting down a pewter pot fit for a guardsman, she rose and sauntered toward the door; stopping there, with one hand on her hip, she looked back.

"Ever see 'im?" she observed, nodding her bonnet at the portrait. "Noticed you appeared hinterested, as if you 'ad!"

"Perhaps!" Steele laughed, not pleasantly. "In my mind's eye, as the poet says."

"Wot the--!" she retorted elegantly. "'Ere's a swell toff to chawf a lidy! 'Owever," reflectively, "I'ave 'eard 'e could 'it 'ard!"

"But that," said the gentleman, indicating the tankard, "could hit harder."

"My hyes; wot's the name of yer missionary friend, ragbags?" to Joe.

"The gentleman's a lawyer, and when I tell you his name is--"

John Steele reached over and stopped the speaker; the woman laughed.

"Perhaps it ayn't syfe to give it!"

Her voice floated back now from the threshold; predominated for a moment later in one of the corners of the bar leading to the street: "Oi soi, you cawn't go in for a 'arf of bitters without a bloomin' graveyard mist comin' up be'ind yer back!" Then the door slammed; the modern prototype of the "roaring girl" vanished, and another voice--hoarse, that of a man--was heard:

"The blarsted fog is coming down fast."

For some time the two men in the little back room sat silent; then one of them leaned over: "She might have asked you that question, eh, Joe?" The speaker's eyes had turned again to the picture.

The smaller man drew back; a shiver seemed to run over him. "They're a long while about the steak," he murmured.

"For your testimony helped to send him over the water, I believe?" went on the other.

"How do you--? I ain't on the stand now, Mr. Steele!" A spark of defiance momentarily came into Dandy Joe's eyes.

"No; no!" John Steele leaned back, half closed his eyes; again pain, fatigue seemed creeping over him. Outside sounded the clicking and clinking of glasses, a staccato of guffaws, tones vivace. "The harm's been done so far as you are concerned; you, as a factor, have disappeared from the case."

"Glad to hear you say so, Mr. Steele. I mean," the other's voice was uncertain, cautious, "that's a matter long since dead and done with. Didn't imagine you ever knew about it; because that was before your time; you weren't even in London then." The keen eyes of the listener rested steadily on the other; seemed to read deeper. "But as for my testimony helping to send him over the water--"

"Or under!" sotto voce.

Joe swallowed. "It was true, every word of it."

"Good!" John Steele spoke almost listlessly. "Always stick by any one who sticks to you,--whether a friend, or a pal, or a patron."

"A patron!" From the other's lips fell an oath; he seemed about to say something but checked himself; the seconds went by.

"But even if there had been something not quite--strictly in accord--which there wasn't"--quickly--"a man couldn't gainsay what had been said," Dandy Joe began.

"He could," indifferently.

"But that would be--"

"Confessing to perjury? Yes."

"Hold on, Mr. Steele!" The man's eyes began to shine with alarm. "I'm not on the---"

"I know. And it wouldn't do any good, if you were."

"You mean--" in spite of himself, the fellow's tones wavered--"because he's under the water?"

"No; I had in mind that even if he hadn't been drowned, your---"

"Wot! Hadn't---"

"A purely hypothetical case! If the sea gave up its dead"--Joe stirred uneasily--"any retraction on your part wouldn't serve him. In the first place, you wouldn't confess; then if you did--which you wouldn't--to employ the sort of Irish bull you yourself used--you would be discredited. And thus, in any contingency," leaning back with folded arms, his head against the wall, "you have become nil!"

"Blest if I follow you, sir!"

"That, also," said John Steele, "doesn't matter. The principal subject of any consequence, relating to you, is the steak, which is now coming." As he spoke, he rose, leaving Dandy Joe alone at the table.

For a time he did not speak; sitting before a cheerless fire, that feebly attempted to assert itself, he looked once or twice toward the door, as if mindful to go out and leave the place.

But for an inexplicable reason he did not do so; there was nothing to be gained here; yet he lingered. Perhaps one of those subtle, illusory influences we do not yet understand, and which sometimes shape the blundering finite will, mysteriously, without conscious volition, was at work. One about to stumble blindly forward, occasionally stops; why, he knows not.

John Steele continued to regard the dark coals; to divers and sundry sounds from the table where the other ate, he seemed oblivious. Once when the proprietor stepped in, he asked, without looking around, for a certain number of grains of quinine with a glass of water; they probably kept it at the bar. Yes, the man always had it on hand and brought it in.

A touch of fever, might he ask, as the visitor took it; nothing to speak of, was the indifferent answer.

Well, the gentleman should have a care; the gentleman did not reply except to ask for the reckoning; the proprietor figured a moment, then departed with the sovereign that had been tossed to the table.

By this time Dandy Joe had pushed back his chair; his dull eyes gleamed with satisfaction; also, perhaps, with a little calculation.

"Thanking you kindly, sir, it's more than I had a right to expect. If ever I can do anything to show--"

"You can't!"

"I don't suppose so," humbly. Joe looked down; he was thinking; a certain matter in which self-interest played no small part had come to mind. John Steele was known to be generous in his services and small in his charges. Joe regarded him covertly. "Asking your pardon for referring to it--but you've helped so many a poor chap--there's an old pal of mine what is down on his luck, and, happenin' across him the other day, he was asking of me for a good lawyer, who could give him straight talk. One moment, sir! He can pay, or soon would be able to, if--"

"I am not at present," Steele experienced a sense of grim humor, "looking for new clients."

"Well, I thought I'd be mentioning the matter, sir, although I hadn't much hopes of him being able to interest the likes of you. You see he's been out of old England for a long time, and was goin' away again, when w'at should he suddenly hear but that his old woman that was, meaning his mother, died and left a tidy bit. A few hundred pounds or so; enough to start a nice, little pub. for him and me to run; only it's in the hands of a trustee, who is waiting for him to appear and claim it."

"You say he has been out of England?" John Steele stopped. "How long?"

"A good many years. There was one or two little matters agin him when he left 'ome; but he has heard that certain offenses may be 'outlawed.' Not that he has much 'ope his'n had, only he wanted to see a lawyer; and find out, in any case, how he could get his money without--"

"The law getting hold of him? What is his name?"

"Tom Rogers."

For some minutes John Steele did not speak; he stood motionless. On the street before the house a barrel-organ began to play; its tones, broken, wheezy, appealed, nevertheless, to the sodden senses of those at the bar:

"Down with the Liberals, Tories,

Parties of all degree."

Dandy Joe smiled, beat time with his hand.

"You can give me," John Steele spoke bruskly, taking from his pocket a note-book, "this Tom Rogers' address."

Joe looked at the other, seemed about to speak on the impulse, but did not; then his hand slowly ceased its motion.

"I, sir--you see, I can't quite do that--for Tom's laying low, you understand. But if you would let him call around quiet-like, on you--"

John Steele replaced the note-book. "On me?" He spoke slowly; Dandy Joe regarded him with small crafty eyes. "I hardly think the case will prove sufficiently attractive."

The other made no answer; looked away thoughtfully; at the same moment the proprietor stepped in. Steele took the change that was laid on the table, leaving a half-crown, which he indicated that Dandy Joe could appropriate.

"Better not think of going now, sir," the proprietor said to John Steele. "Never saw anything like it the way the fog has thickened; a man couldn't get across London to-night to save his neck."

"Couldn't he?" Dandy Joe stepped toward the door. "I'm going to have a try."

A mist blew in; Dandy Joe went out. John Steele waited a moment, then with a perfunctory nod, walked quietly to the front door. The man had not exaggerated the situation; the fog lay before him like a thick yellow blanket. He looked in the direction his late companion had turned; his figure was just discernible; in a moment it would have been swallowed by the fog, when quickly John Steele walked after him.

CHAPTER XVIII

THROUGH THE FOG

The dense veil overhanging the city, while favorable to John Steele in some respects, lessening for the time his own danger, made more difficult the task to which he now set himself. He dared not too closely approach the figure before him, lest he should be seen and his purpose divined; once or twice Dandy Joe looked around, more, perhaps, from habit than any suspicion that he was followed. Then the other, slackening his steps, sometimes held back too far and through caution imperiled his plan by nearly losing sight of Dandy Joe altogether. As they went on with varying pace, the shuffling form ahead seemed to find the way by instinct; crossed unhesitatingly many intersecting thoroughfares; paused only on the verge of a great one.

Here, where opposing currents had met and become congested, utter confusion reigned; from the masses of vehicles of all kinds, constituting a seemingly inextricable blockade, arose the din of hoarse voices. With the fellow's figure a vague swaying shadow before him, John Steele, too, stopped; stared at the dim blotches of light; listened to the anathemas, the angry snapping of whips. Would Dandy Joe plunge into the mêlée; attempt to pass through that tangle of horses and men? Apparently he found discretion the better part of valor and moving back so quickly he almost touched John Steele, he walked down the intersecting avenue.

Several blocks farther on, the turmoil seemed less marked, and here he essayed to cross; by dint of dodging and darting between restless horses he reached the other side. A sudden closing in of cabs and carts midway between curbs held John Steele back; he caught quickly at the bridle of the nearest horse and forced it aside. An expostulating shout, a half-scream from somewhere greeted the action; a whip snapped, stung his cheek. An instant he paused as if to leap up and drag the aggressor from his seat, but instead with closed hands and set face he pushed on; to be blocked again by an importunate cab.

"Turn back; get out of this somehow, cabby!" He heard familiar tones, saw the speaker, Sir Charles, and, by his side--yes, through the curtain of fog, so near he could almost reach out and touch her, he saw as in a flash, Jocelyn Wray!

She, too, saw him, the man in the street, his pale face lifted up, ghost-like, from the mist. A cry fell from her lips, was lost amid other sounds. An instant eyes looked into eyes; hers, dilated; his, unnaturally bright, burning!

Then as in a daze the beautiful head bent toward him; the daintily clad figure leaned forward, the sensitive and trembling lips half parted.

John Steele sprang back, to get free, to get out of there at once! Did she call? he did not know; it might be she had given voice to her surprise, but now only the clatter and uproar could be heard. In the fog, however, her face seemed still to follow; confused, for a moment, he did not heed his way. Something struck him--a wheel? He half fell, recovered himself, managed to reach the curb.

He was conscious now of louder shoutings; of the sting on his cheek; of the traffic, drifting on--slowly. Then he, too, started to walk away, in the opposite direction; it mattered little whither he bent his footsteps now. Dandy Joe had disappeared; the hope of attaining his end through him, of being led to the retreat of one he had so long desired to find, had proved illusive. The last moment's halt had enabled him to escape, to fade from view like a will-o'-the-wisp.

John Steele did not go far in mere aimless fashion; leaning against a wall he strove once more to plan, but ever as he did so, through his thought the girl's fair face, looking out from enshrouding lace, intruded. Again he felt the light of her eyes, all the bitterness of spirit their surprise, consternation, had once more awakened in him.

He looked out at the wagons, the carts, the nondescript vehicles of every description; but a moment before she had been there,--so near; he had caught beneath filmy white the glitter of gold,--her hair, the only bright thing in that murk and gloom. He recalled how he had once sat beside her at the opera. How different was this babel, this grinding and crunching of London's thundering wheels!

But around her had always been dreams that had led him into strange byways, through dangerous, though flowery paths! To what end? To see her start, her eyes wide with involuntary dread, shrinking? Could he not thus interpret that look he had seen by the flare of a carriage lamp, when she had caught sight of him?

Dread of him? It seemed the crowning mockery; his blood surged faster; he forgot his purpose, when a figure coming out of a public house, through one of the doors near which he had halted, caught his attention. Dandy Joe, a prodigal with unexpected riches, wiped his lips as he sauntered past John Steele and continued his way, lurching a little.

How long did Steele walk after him? The distance across the city was far; groping, occasionally stumbling, it seemed interminable now. Once or twice

Dandy Joe lost his way, and jocularly accosted passers-by to inquire. At Seven Dials he experienced difficulty in determining which one of the miserable streets radiating as from a common hub, would lead him in the desired direction; but, after looking hastily at various objects--a barber's post, a metal plate on a wall--he selected his street. Narrow, dark, it wormed its way through a cankered and little-traversed part of old London.

For a time they two seemed the only pedestrians that had ventured forth that night in a locality so uninviting. On either side the houses pressed closer upon them. Touching a wall here and there, John Steele experienced the vague sensation that he had walked that way on other occasions, long, long ago. Or was it only a bad dream that again stirred him? Through the gulch-like passage swept a cold draft of air; it made little rifts in the fog; showed an entrance, a dim light. At the same time the sound of the footsteps in front abruptly ceased.

For a few minutes Steele waited; he looked toward the place Dandy Joe had entered. It was well-known to him, and, what seemed more important, to Mr. Gillett; the latter would remember it in connection with the 'Frisco Pet; presumably turn to it as a likely spot to search for him who had been forced to leave Captain Forsythe's home. That contingency--nay, probability--had to be considered; the one person he most needed to find had taken refuge in one of the places he would have preferred not to enter. But no time must be lost hesitating; he had to choose. Dismissing all thought of danger from without, thinking only of what lay before him within, he moved quickly forward and tried the door.

It yielded; had Dandy Joe left it unfastened purposely to lure him within, or had his potations made him unmindful? The man outside neither knew nor cared; the mocking consciousness that he had turned that knob before, knew how to proceed, held him. He entered, felt his way in the darkness through winding passages, downward, avoiding a bad step--did he remember even that?

How paltry details stood out! The earthen floor still drowned the sound of footsteps; the narrow hall took the same turns; led on and on in devious fashion until he could hear, like the faint hum of bees, the distant rumble from the great thoroughfares, somewhere above, that paralleled the course of the river. At the same time a slant of light like a sword, from the crack of a door, gleamed on the dark floor before him; he stepped toward it; the low sound of men's tones could be heard--Joe's; a strange voice! no, a familiar one!--that caused the listener's every fiber to vibrate.

"And what did you say, when he pumped you for the cote?"

"That you would rather call on him."

"And then he cared nought for the job? You're sure"--anxiously--"he wasn't playing to find out?"

The other answered jocosely and walked away; a door closed behind him. For a time the stillness remained unbroken; then a low rattle, as of dice on a table, caused John Steele to glance through a crevice. What he saw seemed to decide him to act quickly; he lifted a latch and stepped in. As he did so a huge man with red hair sprang to his feet; from one great hand the dice fell to the floor; his shaggy jowl drooped. Casting over his shoulder the swift glance of an entrapped animal, he seemed about to leap backward to escape by a rear entrance when the voice of the intruder arrested his purpose, momentarily held him.

"Oh, I'm alone! There are no police outside." He spoke in the dialect of the pick-purse and magsman. To prove it, John Steele stooped and locked the door.

The small bloodshot eyes lighted with wonder; the heavy brutish jaws began to harden. "Alone?"

The other tossed the key; it fell at the man's feet; John Steele walked over to the opposite door and shot a heavy bolt there. "Looks as if it would hold," he said in thieves' argot as he turned around.

"Are ye a gaby?" The red-headed giant stared ominously at him.

"On the contrary," coolly, "I know very well what I am doing."

A question interlarded with oaths burst from the other's throat; John Steele regarded the man quietly. "I should think it apparent what I want!" he answered. As he spoke, he sat down. "It is you," bending his bright, resolute eyes on the other.

"And you've come alone?" He drew up his ponderous form.

John Steele smiled. "I assure you I welcomed the opportunity."

"You won't long." The great fists closed. "Do you know what I am going to do to you?"

"I haven't any curiosity," still clinging to thieves' jargon or St. Giles Greek. "But I'm sure you won't play me the trick you did the last time I saw you."

The fellow shot his head near; in his look shone a gleam of recognition. "You're the swell cove who wanted to palaver that night when--"

"You tried to rob me of my purse?"

John Steele laughed; his glance lingered on his bulky adversary with odd, persistent exhilaration, as if after all that had gone before, this contest royal, which promised to become one of sheer brute strength, awoke to its utmost a primal fighting force in him. "Do you know the penalty for attempting that game, Tom Rogers, alias Tom-o'-the-Road; alias---"

The man fell back, in his eyes a look of ferocious wonderment. "Who are you? By---!" he said.

"John Steele."

"John Steele?" The bloodshot eyes became slightly vacuous. "The--? Then you used him," indicating savagely the entrance at the back, "for a duck to uncover?" Steele nodded. "And you're the one who's been so long at my heels?" Rage caused the hot blood to suffuse the man's face. "I'll burke you for that."

John Steele did not stir; for an instant his look, confident, assured, seemed to keep the other back. "How? With the lead, or--"

The fellow lifted his hairy fists. "Those are all I--"

"In that case--" Steele took the weapon, on which his hand had rested, from his pocket; rising with alacrity he placed it on a rickety stand behind him. "You have me a little outclassed; about seventeen stone, I should take it; barely turn thirteen, myself. However," tossing his coat in the corner, "you look a little soft; hardly up to what you were when you got the belt for the heavy-weight championship. Do you remember? The 'Frisco Pet went against you; but he was only a low, ignorant sailor and had let himself get out of form. You beat him, beat him," John Steele's eyes glittered; he touched the other on the arm, "though he fought seventeen good rounds! You stamped the heart out of him, Tom."

The red-headed giant's arms fell to his side. "How do you--"

"I was there!" An odd smile crossed Steele's determined lips. "Lost a little money on that battle. Recall the fourteenth round? He nearly had you; but you played safe in the fifteenth, and then--you sent him down--down," John Steele's voice died away. "It was a long time before he got up," he added, almost absently.

The listener's face had become a study; perplexity mingled with other conflicting emotions. "You know all that--?"

"And all the rest! How for you the fascination of the road became greater than that of the ring; how the old wildness would crop out; how the highway drew you, until--"

"See here, what's your little game? Straight now; quick! You come here, without the police, why?"

John Steele's reply was to the point; he stated exactly what he wanted and what he meant that the other should give him. As the fellow heard, he breathed harder; he held himself in with difficulty.

"And so that's what you've come for, Mister?" he said, a hoarse guffaw falling from the coarse lips. John Steele answered quietly. "And you think there is any chance of your getting it? May I be asking," with an evil grin, "how you expect to make me, Tom Rogers," bringing down his great fist, "do your bidding?"

"In the first place by assuring you no harm shall come to you. It is in my power to avert that, in case you comply. In the second place, you will be given enough sovereigns to--"

"Quids, eh? Let me have sight of them, Mister. We might talk better."

"Do you think I'd bring them here, Tom-o'-the-Road? No, no!" bruskly.

"That settles it." The other made a gesture, contemptuous, dissenting.

John Steele's manner changed; he turned suddenly on the fellow like lightning. "In the next place by giving you your choice of doing what I ask, or of being turned over to the traps."

"The traps!" The other fellow's face became contorted. "You mean that you--"

"Will give you up for that little job, unless--"

For answer the man launched his huge body forward, with fierce swinging fists.

What happened thereafter was at once brutish, terrible, Homeric; the fellow's reserves of strength seemed immense; sheer animal rage drove him; he ran amuck with lust to kill. He beat, rushed, strove to close. His opponent's lithe body evaded a clutch that might have ended the contest. John Steele fought without sign of anger, like a machine, wonderfully trained; missing no point, regardless of punishment. He knew that if he went down once, all rules of battle would be discarded; a powerful blow sent him staggering to the wall; he leaned against it an instant; waited, with the strong, impelling look people had noticed on his face when he was fighting in a different way, in the courts.

The other came at him, muttering; the mill had unduly prolonged itself; he would end it. His fist struck at that face so elusive; but crashed against the wall; like a flash Steele's arm lifted. The great form staggered, fell.

Quickly, however, it rose and the battle was resumed. Now, despite John Steele's vigilance, the two came together. Tom Rogers' arm wound round him with suffocating power; strove, strained, to hurl him to earth. But the other's perfect training, his orderly living, saved him at that crucial moment; his strength of endurance lasted; with a great effort he managed to tear himself loose and at the same time with a powerful upper stroke to send Rogers once more to the floor. Again, however, he got to his feet; John Steele's every muscle ached; his shoulder was bleeding anew. The need for acting quickly, if he should hope to conquer, pressed on him; fortunately Rogers in his blind rage was fighting wildly. John Steele endured blow after blow; then, as through a mist, he found at length the opening he sought; an instant's opportunity on which all depended.

Every fiber of his physical being responded; he threw himself forward, the weight of his body, the force of a culminating impetus, went into his fist; it hit heavily; full on the point of the chin beneath the brutal mouth. Tom Rogers' head shot back as if he had received the blow of a hammer; he threw up his arms; this time he lay where he struck the ground.

John Steele swayed; with an effort he sustained himself. Was it over? Still Rogers did not move; Steele stooped, felt his heart; it beat slowly. Mechanically, as if hardly knowing what he did, John Steele began to count; "Time!" Rogers continued to lie like a log; his mouth gaped; the blow, in the parlance of the ring, had been a "knock-out"; or, in this case, a quid pro quo. Yes, the last, but without referee or spectators! The prostrate man did stir now; he groaned; John Steele touched him with his foot.

"Get up," he said.

The other half-raised himself and regarded the speaker with dazed eyes. "What for?"

John Steele went to the stand, picked up his revolver, and then sat down at a table. "You're as foul a fighter as you ever were," he said contemptuously.

CHAPTER XIX

THE LAST SHIFT

The candle burned low; it threw now on grimy floor and wall the shadows of the two men, one seated at the table, the other not far from it. Before John Steele lay paper and ink, procured from some niche. He had ceased writing; for the moment he leaned back, his vigilant gaze on the figure near-by. From a corner of the room the rasping sound of a rat, gnawing, broke the stillness, then suddenly ceased.

"Where were you on the night this woman, Amy Gerard, was found dead?"

A momentary expression of surprise, of alarm, crossed the bruised and battered face; it was succeeded by an angry suspicion that glowed from the evil eyes. "You're not trying to fix that job on---"

"You? No."

"Then what did you follow him here for, to pump me? The Yankee that got transported is--"

"As alive as when he stepped before you in the ring!"

"Alive?" The fellow stared. "Not in England? It was death for him to come back!"

"Never mind his whereabouts."

The man looked at Steele closer. "Blame, if there isn't something about you that puzzles me," he said.

"What?" laconically.

The fellow shook his head. "And so he's hired you?"

"Not exactly. Although I may say I represent him."

"Well, he got a good one. You know how to use your fists, Mister."

"Better than this 'Frisco Pet did once, eh, Tom?" The man frowned. "But to return to the subject in hand. That question you seemed afraid to answer just now was superfluous; I know where you were the night the woman was shot."

"You do?"

"Yes; you were--" John Steele leaned forward and said something softly.

"How'd you find that out?" asked the man.

"The 'Frisco Pet knew where you were all the time; but did not speak, because he did not wish to get you into trouble. Also, because he did not know, then, what he long afterward learned,--indirectly!--that you could have cleared him!"

"Indirectly? I? What do you--?"

"Through your once having dropped a few words. Wine in, wits out!"

The fellow scowled; edged his chair closer.

"Keep where you are!" John Steele's hand touched the revolver now on the table before him; even as it did so, the room seemed to sway, and it was only by a strong effort of will he kept his attention on the matter in hand, fought down the dizziness. "And let's get through with this! I don't care to waste much more of my time on you."

"You're sure nothing will happen to me, if--" The man watched him closer.

"This paper need never be made public."

"Then what--"

"That's my business. It might be useful in certain contingencies."

"Such as the police discovering he hadn't gone to Davy Jones' locker?" shrewdly.

John Steele's answer was short, as if he found this verbal contest trite, paltry, after the physical struggle that had preceded it.

"And what am I to get if I do what you--" The pupils of the fellow's eyes, fastened on him, were now like pin-points.

The other smiled grimly; this bargaining and trafficking with such a man, in a place so foul! It seemed grotesque, incongruous; and yet was, withal, so momentous. He knew just what Rogers should say; what he would force him to do! In his overwrought state he overlooked one or two points that would not have escaped him at another time: a certain craftiness, or low cunning that played occasionally on that disfigured face.

"What did you say I was to get if--"

"You shall have funds to take you out of the country, and I will engage to get and forward to you the money left in trust. The alternative," he bent forward, "about fifteen years, if the traps--"

The fellow pondered; at last he answered. For a few minutes then John Steele wrote, looking up between words. His head bent now closer to the paper, then drew back from it, as if through a slight uncertainty of vision or because of the dim light. The fellow's eyes, watching him, lowered.

"You know--none better!--that on that particular night some one else--some one besides the 'Frisco Pet--entered your mother's house?"

Oaths mingled with low filchers' slang; but the reply was forthcoming; other questions, too, were answered tentatively; sometimes at length, with repulsive fullness of detail. The speaker hesitated over words, shot sharp, short looks at the other; from the hand that wrote, to the fingers near that other object,--strong, firm fingers that seemed ready to leap; ready to act on any emergency. Unless--a shadow appeared to pass over the broad, white brow, the motionless hand to waver, ever so little. Then quickly the hand moved, rested on the brown handle of the weapon, enveloped it with light careless grasp.

"You can state of your own knowledge what happened next?" John Steele spoke sharply; the fellow's red brows suddenly lifted.

"Oh, yes," he replied readily.

John Steele's manner became shorter; his questions were put fast; he forced quick replies. He not only seemed striving to get through his task as soon as possible; but always to hold the other's attention, to permit his brain no chance to wander from the subject to any other. But the fellow seemed now to have become as tractable as before he had been sullen, stubborn; gave his version in his own vernacular, always keenly attentive, observant of the other's every motion. His strength had apparently returned; he seemed little the worse for his late encounter. At length came an interval; just for an instant John Steele's eyes shut; the fingers that had held the pen closed on the edge of the table. A quick passing expression of ferocity hovered at the corners of the observer's thick lips; he got up; at the same time John Steele rose and stepped abruptly back.

"You know how to write your name?" His voice was firm, unwavering; the revolver had disappeared from the table and lay now in his pocket.

"All right, gov'ner!" The other spoke with alacrity. "I'm game; a bargain is a bargain, and I'll take your word for it," leaning over and laboriously tracing a few letters on the paper. "You'll do your part. You'll find me square and above board, although you did use me a little rough. There, here's your affadavy."

John Steele moved back to a corner of the room and pulled a wire; in some far-away place a bell rang faintly. "Are----," he spoke a woman's name, obviously a sobriquet, "and her daughter still here?"

"How?"

"Never mind; answer."

"Yes, they're here, gov'ner. You'll want them for witnesses, I suppose. Well, I'll not be gainsaying you." His tones were loud; conveyed a sense of rough heartiness; the other made no reply.

Not long after, the paper, duly witnessed, lay on the table; the landlady and her daughter had gone; John Steele only waited for the ink to dry. He had no blotter, or sand; the fluid was old, thick; the principal signature in its big strokes, with here and there a splutter, would be unintelligible if the paper were folded now. So he lingered; both men were silent; a few tense minutes passed. John Steele leaned against the wall; his temples throbbed; the fog seemed creeping into the room and yet the door was closed. He moved toward the paper; still maintaining an aspect of outward vigilance, took it and held it before him as if to examine closer.

The other said nothing, made no movement. When the women had come in, his accents had been almost too frank; the gentleman had called on a little matter of business; he, Tom Rogers, had voluntarily signed this little paper, and they could bear witness to the fact. Now all that profanely free air had left him; he stood like a statue, his lips compressed; his eyes alone were alive, speaking, alert.

John Steele folded the paper and placed it in an inside pocket. The other suddenly breathed heavily; John Steele, looking at him, walked to the door leading to the street. He put his hand on the key and was about to turn it, but paused. Something without held his attention,--a crunching sound as of a foot on a pebble. It abruptly revived misgivings that had assailed him before entering the place, that he had felt as a vague weight while dealing with the fellow. The police agent! Time had passed, too great an interval, though he had hastened, hastened as best he might, struggling with his own growing weakness, the other's reviving power.

Again the sound! Involuntarily he turned his head; it was only an instant's inattention, but Tom Rogers had been waiting for it. Springing behind in a flash, he seized John Steele by the throat. It was a deadly, terrible grip; the fingers pressed harder; the other strove, but slowly fell. As dizziness began to merge into oblivion, Rogers, without releasing his hold, bent over.

"You fool! Did you think I would let you get away with the paper? That I couldn't see you were about done for?"

He looked at the white face; started to unbutton the coat; as he reached in, his attention was suddenly arrested; he threw back his head.

"The traps!"

Voices below resounded without.

"So that was your game! Well," savagely, "I think I have settled with you."

He had but time to run to the rear door, unbolt it and dash out, when a crashing of woodwork filled the place, and Mr. Gillett looked in.

CHAPTER XX

THE PAPER

When John Steele began to recover, he was dimly aware that he was in a four-wheeler which rattled along slowly through streets, now slightly more discernible; by his side sat a figure that stirred when he did; spoke in crisp, official accents. He, Mr. Steele, would kindly not place any further obstacles in the way of justice being done; it was useless to attempt that; the police agent had come well armed, and, moreover, had taken the precaution for this little journey of providing a cab in front and one behind, containing those who knew how to act should the necessity arise.

John Steele heard these words without answering; his throat pained him; he could scarcely swallow; his head seemed bound around as by a tight, inflexible band. The cool air, however, gradually revived him; he drank it in gratefully and strove to think. A realization of what had occurred surged through his brain,--the abrupt attack at the door; the arrival of the police agent.

Furtively the prisoner felt his pocket; the memorandum book containing the paper that had cost so much was gone; he looked at the agent. Had it been shifted to Mr. Gillett's possession, or, dimly he recalled his assailant's last words, had Rogers succeeded in snatching the precious evidence from his breast before escaping? In the latter case, it had, undoubtedly, ere this, been destroyed; in the former, it would, presumably, soon be transferred to the police agent's employer. To regain the paper, if it existed, would be no light task; yet it was the pivot upon which John Steele's fortunes hung. The principal signer was, in all likelihood, making his way out of London now; he would, in a few hours, reach the sea, and after that disappear from the case. At any rate, John Steele could have nothing to hope from him in the future; the opportune or inopportune appearance of the police agent would savor of treachery to him. John Steele moved, quickly, impatiently; but a hand, swung carelessly behind him, moved also,--a hand that held something hard.

Thereafter he remained outwardly quiescent; resistance on his part, and the consequences that would ensue, might not be displeasing to his chief enemy; it would settle the case in short and summary fashion. Justification for extreme proceedings would be easily forthcoming and there would be none to answer for John Steele.

Where were they going? John Steele could not surmise; he saw, however that they had left behind the neighborhood of hovels, narrow passages and byways, and traversed now one of the principal circuses. There the street traffic moved smoothly; they seemed but an unimportant part of an endless procession which they soon left to turn into a less public, more aristocratic highway. A short distance down this street, the carriages suddenly stopped before an eminently respectable and sedate front, and, not long after, John Steele, somewhat to his surprise, found himself in Lord Ronsdale's rooms and that person's presence.

The nobleman had been forewarned of John Steele's coming. He sat behind a high desk, his figure and part of his face screened by its massive back. One drawer of the desk was slightly opened. What could be seen of his features appeared sharper than usual, as if the inner virulence, the dark hidden passions smoldering in his breast had at length stamped their impression on the outer man. When he first spoke his tones were more irascible, less icily imperturbable, than they had been hitherto. They seemed to tell of a secret tension he had long been laboring under; but the steady cold eyes looked out from behind the wood barrier with vicious assurance.

The police agent he addressed first; his services could be dispensed with for the present; he should, however, remain in the hall with his men. Mr. Gillett looked from the speaker to him he had brought there and after a moment turned and obeyed; but the instant's hesitation seemed to say that he began to realize there was more to the affair than he had fathomed.

"There is no need for many words between us, Mr. Steele." Lord Ronsdale's accents were poignant and sharp. "Had you listened to what Mr. Gillett, on my behalf, would have said to you that night in the gardens at Strathorn House, we might, possibly, both of us, have been saved some little annoyance. We now start at about where we were before that little contretemps."

John Steele silently looked at Lord Ronsdale; his brain had again become clear; his thoughts, lucid. The ride through the cool and damp air, this outré encounter at the end of the journey, had acted as a tonic on jaded sense and faculty. He saw distinctly, heard very plainly; his ideas began to marshal themselves logically. He could have laughed at Lord Ronsdale, but the situation was too serious; the weakness of his defenses too obvious. Proofs, proofs, proofs, were what the English jury demanded, and where were his? He could build up a story; yes, but--if he could have known what had taken place between Mr. Gillett and this man a few minutes before, when the police agent had stepped in first and tarried here a brief period before ushering him in!

Had Mr. Gillett delivered to his noble patron the memorandum book and other articles filched from John Steele's pockets? That partly opened drawer--what did it contain? The nobleman's hand lingered on the edge of it; with an effort the other resisted allowing his glance to rest there.

He even refused to smile when Lord Ronsdale, after a sharper look, asked him to be seated; he seemed to sift and weigh the pros and cons of the invitation in a curious, calm fashion; as if he felt himself there in some impersonal capacity for the purpose of solving a difficult catechetical problem.

"Yes; I think I will." He sat down in a stiff, straight-backed chair; it may be he felt the need of holding in reserve all his physical force, of not refusing to rest, even here.

Lord Ronsdale's glance narrowed; he hesitated an instant. "To go back to Strathorn House--a very beautiful place to go back to," his tones for the moment lapsed to that high pitch they sometimes assumed, "Mr Gillett had there received from me certain instructions. Whatever you once were," seeming not to notice the other's expression, "you have since by your own efforts attained much. How--?" His brows knit as at something inexplicable. "But the fact remained, was perhaps considered. Exposure would have meant some--unpleasantness for your friends." The eyes of the two men met; those of Lord Ronsdale were full of sardonic meaning. "Friends who had trusted you; who," softly, "had admitted you to their firesides, not knowing--" he broke off. "They," he still adhered to the plural, "would have been deeply shocked, pained; would still be if they should learn--"

"If?" John Steele did manage to contain himself, but it was with an effort; perhaps he saw again through the fog a girl's face, white and accusing, which had appeared; vanished. "You spoke of certain instructions?" he even forced himself to say.

"Mr. Gillett, in the garden at Strathorn House, was authorized by me to offer you one chance of avoiding exposure, and," deliberately, "the attendant consequences; you were to be suffered to leave London, this country, with the stipulation that you should never return." John Steele shifted slightly. "You did not expect this," quickly, "you had not included that contingency in your calculations?"

"I confess," in an even, emotionless voice, "your lordship's complaisance amazes me."

"And you would have accepted the alternative?" The nobleman's accents were now those of the service, diplomatic; they were concise but measured.

"Why discuss what could never have been considered?" was the brusk answer.

Lord Ronsdale frowned. "We are still fencing; we will waste no more time." Perhaps the other's manner, assured, contemptuously distant, goaded him; perhaps he experienced anew all that first violent, unreasoning anger against this man whose unexpected coming to London had plunged him into an unwelcome and irritating role. "That alternative is still open. Refuse, and--you will be in the hands of the authorities to-night. Resist--" His glittering eyes left no doubt whatever as to his meaning.

"I shall not resist," said John Steele. "But--I refuse." He spoke recklessly, regardlessly.

"In that case--" Lord Ronsdale half rose; his face looked drawn but determined; he reached as if to touch a bell. "You force the issue, and--"

"One moment." As he spoke John Steele stepped toward the fireplace; he gazed downward at a tiny white ash on the glowing coals; a little film that might have been--paper? "In a matter so important we may consider a little longer, lest," still regarding the hearth, "there may be after-regrets." His words even to himself sounded puerile; but what they led to had more poignancy; he lifted now his keen glowing eyes. "In one little regard I did your lordship an injustice."

"In what way?" The nobleman had been studying him closely, had followed the direction of his glance; noted almost questioningly what it had rested on--the coals, or vacancy?

"In supposing that you yourself murdered Amy Gerard," came the unexpected response. The other started violently. "Your lordship will forgive the assumption in view of what occurred on a certain stormy night at sea, when a drowning wretch clung with one hand to a gunwale, and you, in answer to his appeal for succor, bent over and--"

"It's a lie!" The words fell in a sharp whisper.

"What?" John Steele's laugh sounded mirthlessly. "However, we will give a charitable interpretation to the act; the boat was already overcrowded; one more might have endangered all. Call it an impulse of self-preservation. Self-preservation," he repeated; "the struggle of the survival of the fittest! Let the episode go. Especially as your lordship incidentally did me a great service; a very great service." The other stared at him. "I should have looked at it only in that light, and then it would not have played me the trick it did of affording a false hypothesis for a certain conclusion. Your lordship knows what I mean, how the true facts in this case of Amy Gerard have come to light?"

John Steele's glance was straight, direct; if the other had the paper, had read it, he would know.

Lord Ronsdale looked toward the bell, hesitated. "I think you had better tell me," he said at last.

"If your lordship did not kill the woman--if the 'Frisco Pet did not, then who did?" Ronsdale leaned forward just in the least; his eyes seemed to look into the other's as if to ask how much, just what, he had learned. John Steele studied the nobleman with a purpose of his own. "Why, she killed herself," he said suddenly.

"How?" The nobleman uttered this word, then stopped; John Steele waited. Had Lord Ronsdale been surprised at his knowledge? He could hardly tell, from his manner, whether or not he had the affidavit and had read it.

"How--interesting!" The nobleman was willing to continue the verbal contest a little longer; that seemed a point gained. "May I ask how it occurred?"

"Oh, it is all very commonplace! Your lordship had received a threatening letter and called on the woman. She wanted money; you refused. She already had a husband living in France, a ruined gambler of the Bourse, but had tricked you into thinking she was your wife. You had discovered the deception and discarded her. From a music-hall singer she had gone down-- down, until she, once beautiful, courted, had become a mere--what she was, associate of one like Dandy Joe, cunning, unscrupulous. At your refusal to become the victim of their blackmailing scheme, she in her anger seized a weapon; during the struggle, it was accidentally discharged."

Was Lord Ronsdale asking himself how the other had learned this? If Rogers had escaped with the paper, John Steele knew Ronsdale might well wonder that the actual truth should have been discovered; he would not, under those circumstances, even be aware of the existence of a witness of the tragedy. But was Lord Ronsdale assuming a manner, meeting subtlety with subtlety? John Steele went on quietly, studying his enemy with close, attentive gaze.

"At sound of the shot, Joe, who had been waiting below in the kitchen with the landlady, rushed up-stairs. You explained how it happened; were willing enough to give money now to get away quietly without being dragged into the affair. The dead woman's confederate, greedy for gain even at such a moment, would have helped you; but there was a difficulty: would the police accept the story of suicide? There were signs of a struggle. At that instant some one entered the house, came stumbling up the stairs; it was the-- 'Frisco Pet."

John Steele paused; his listener sat stiff, immovable. "Joe hurried you out, toward a rear exit, but not before," leaning slightly toward Lord Ronsdale, "an impression of your face, pale, drawn, had vaguely stamped itself on the befuddled brain," bitterly, "of the fool-brute. You lost no time in making your escape; little was said between you and Joe; but he proved amenable to your suggestion; the way out of the difficulty was found. He hated the Pet, who had once or twice handled him roughly for abusing this poor creature. You gave Joe money to have the landlady's testimony agree with his; she never got that money," meaningly, "but gave the desired evidence. Joe had found out something."

Once more the speaker stopped; there remained a crucial test. If Lord Ronsdale had the paper, what John Steele was about to say would cause him no surprise; he would be prepared for it. The words fell sharply:

"The landlady's son, Tom Rogers, was at the time in the house, in hiding from the police. He was concealed above in a small room or garret; through a stove-pipe opening, disused, he looked down into the sitting-room below and heard, saw all!"

The effect was instantaneous, magical; Lord Ronsdale sprang to his feet; John Steele looked at him, at the wavering face, the uncertain eyes. No doubt existed now in his mind; Gillett had not secured the paper, or he would have given it to his patron when they were alone. That fact was patent; the document was gone, irretrievably; there could be no hope of recovering it. The bitter knowledge that it had really once existed would not serve John Steele long. But with seeming resolution he went on: "I had the story from his own lips," deliberately, "put in the form of an affidavit, duly signed and witnessed."

"You did?" Lord Ronsdale stared at him a long time. "This is a subterfuge."

"It is true."

"Where--is the paper?"

"Not in my pocket."

The other considered. "You mean it is in a safe place?"

"One would naturally take care of such a document."

"You did not have any such paper at Strathorn."

"No?" John Steele smiled but he did not feel like smiling. "Not there certainly."

"I mean no such paper existed then, or you would have taken advantage of it."

John Steele did not answer; he looked at the drawer. The affidavit was not there; but something else was.

"You are resourceful, that is all."

Lord Ronsdale had now quite recovered himself; he sank back into his chair. "You have, out of fancy, constructed a libelous theory; one that you can not prove; one that you would be laughed at for advancing. A cock-and-bull story about a witness who was not a witness; a paper that doesn't exist, that never existed."

A sound at the door caused him to turn sharply; a knocking had passed unheeded. The door opened, closed. Mr. Gillett, a troubled, perturbed look on his face, stood now just within. "Your lordship!"

"Well?" the nobleman's manner was peremptory.

The police agent, however, came forward slowly. "I have here something that one of our men has just turned over to me." John Steele started; but neither of the others noticed. "He found it at the last place we were; evidently it had been dropped by the fellow who was there and who fled at our coming." As he spoke, he stepped nearer the desk, in his hand a paper.

"What is it?" Lord Ronsdale demanded testily.

Mr. Gillett did not at once answer; he looked at John Steele; the latter stood like a statue; only his eyes were turned toward the nobleman, to the thin aristocratic hand yet resting on the edge of the drawer.

"If your lordship will glance at it?" said Mr. Gillett, proffering the sheet.

The nobleman did so; his face changed; his eyes seemed unable to leave the paper. Suddenly he gave a smothered explanation; tore the sheet once, and started up, took a step toward the fire.

Illustration: Stop! The voice was John Steele's Page

"Stop!" The voice was John Steele's; he stood now next to the partly-opened drawer, in his hand that which had been concealed there, something bright, shining. Lord Ronsdale wheeled, looked at the weapon and into the eyes behind it. "Place those two bits of paper there--on the edge of the desk!"

CHAPTER XXI

A CONDITION

Lord Ronsdale hesitated; his thin jaws were set so that the bones of the cheek showed; his eyes gleamed. When he did move it was as if blindly, precipitately, to carry out his first impulse.

"I wouldn't!" What John Steele held vaguely included, in the radius of its possibilities, Mr. Gillett. "Unless--"

"You wouldn't dare!" Lord Ronsdale trembled, but with impotent passion, not fear. "It would be--"

"Self-defense! The paper would remain--full vindication. In fact the paper already is mine. Whether I kill you or not is merely incidental. And to tell you the truth I don't much care how you decide!"

Again Lord Ronsdale seemed almost to forget caution; almost, but not quite; perhaps he was deterred by the look on John Steele's face, scornful, mocking, as half-inviting him to cast all prudence to the winds. This bit of evidence that he had not calculated upon, it was hard to give it up; but no other course remained. Besides, another, Gillett, knew of its existence; Lord Ronsdale felt he could not depend on that person in an emergency of this kind; the police agent's manner was not reassuring. He seemed inclined to be more passive than aggressive; perhaps he had been somewhat overcome by this unexpected revelation and the deep waters he who boasted of an "eminently respectable and reputable agency" had unwittingly drifted into; in climaxes of this character one's thoughts are likely to center on self, to the exclusion of patron or employer, however noble. The police agent looked at Ronsdale and waited to see what he would do.

The nobleman moved toward the desk; the paper fluttered from his cold fingers; when once more John Steele buttoned his coat the affidavit had again found lodgment in his waistcoat pocket.

It seemed a tame, commonplace end; but it was the end; all three men knew it. John Steele's burning glance swept from Lord Ronsdale to Gillett; lingered with mute contemplation. What now remained to be done should be easily, it seemed almost too easily, accomplished. He felt like one lingering on the stage after the curtain had gone down; the varied excitement, the fierce play of emotion was over; the actors hardly appeared interesting.

What he said was for Lord Ronsdale alone; after Gillett had gone, he laid down a condition. In certain respects it was a moment of triumph; but he experienced no exultation, only a supreme weariness, an anxiety to be done with the affair, to go. But the one point had first to be made, emphasized; to be accepted by the other violently, quietly, resignedly,--John Steele did not care what his attitude might be; what he chiefly felt was that he did not wish to waste much time on him.

"And if I refuse to let you dictate in a purely private concern?" Lord Ronsdale, white with passion, had answered.

"The end will be the same for you. As matters stand, Sir Charles no doubt thinks still that you would make a desirable parti for his niece. His wife, Lady Wray, unquestionably shares that opinion. Their combined influence might in time prevail, and Jocelyn Wray yield to their united wishes. This misfortune," with cutting deadliness of tone, "it is obvious must be averted. You will consent to withdraw all pretensions in that direction, or you will force me to make public this paper. A full exposition of the case I think would materially affect Sir Charles and Lady Wray's attitude as to the desirability of an alliance between their family and yours."

"And yourself? You forget," with a sneer, "how it would affect you!"

"Myself!" John Steele laughed. "You fool! Do you imagine I would hesitate for that reason?"

The nobleman looked at him, at the glowing, contemptuous eyes. "Hesitate? Perhaps not! You love her yourself, and--"

John Steele stepped toward him. "Stop, or--I have once been almost on the point of killing you to-night--don't--" he broke off. "The condition? You consent or not?"

"And if I--? You would--?"

"Keep your cowardly secret? Yes!"

To this the other had replied; of necessity the scene had dragged along a little farther; then John Steele found himself on the stairway, going down.

It was over, this long, stubborn contest; he hardly heard or saw a cab drive up and stop before the house as he went out to the street, was scarcely conscious of some one leaving it, some one about to enter who suddenly stopped at sight of him and exclaimed eagerly, warmly. He was not surprised; with apathy he listened to the new-comer's words; rambling, disconnected, about a letter that had intercepted him at Brighton and brought him post-haste to London.

A letter? John Steele had entered the cab; he sank back; when had he written a letter? Weeks ago; he looked at this face, familiar, far-off; the fog was again rising around him. He could hardly see; he was glad he did not have to stir; he seemed to breathe with difficulty.

"Where--are we going?"

"To Rosemary Villa."

"I--should prefer--my own chambers"--John Steele spoke with an effort--"it is nearer--and I'm a bit done up. Besides, after a little rest, there are--some business matters--to be attended to--that will need looking after as soon as--"

His head fell forward; Captain Forsythe looked at him; called up loudly, excitedly to the driver.

CHAPTER XXII

NEAR THE RIVER

A dubious sort of day, one that seemed vainly trying to appear cheerful! A day that threw out half-promises, that showed tentatively on the sky a mottled blur where the sun should have been! On such a day, a month after that night in Lord Ronsdale's rooms, Captain Forsythe, calling on John Steele, found himself admitted to the sitting-room. While waiting for an answer to his request to see Mr. Steele, he gazed disapprovingly around him. The rooms were partly dismantled; a number of boxes littering the place indicating preparations to move. Captain Forsythe surveyed these cases, more or less filled; then he shook his head and lighted a cigar. But as he smoked he seemed asking himself a question; he had not yet found the answer when a footstep was heard and the subject of his ruminations entered the room. John Steele's face was paler than it had been; thinner, like that of a man who had recently suffered some severe illness.

"Ah, Forsythe!" he said, with an assumption of cheeriness. "So good of you!"

"That's all very well," was the answer. "But what about those?" With his cigar he indicated vaguely the boxes.

"Those? Not yet all packed, are they? Lazy beggars, your London servants, just before leaving you!" he laughed.

"See here!" Forsythe looked at him. "You're not well enough yet to--"

"Never felt better!"

"No chance to get you to change your mind, I suppose?"

"Not in the least!"

For a few moments Forsythe said nothing; then, "Weed?" he asked, offering Steele a cigar.

"Don't believe I'll begin just yet a while."

"Oh!" significantly. "Quite fit, eh?" Forsythe's tone sounded, in the least, scoffing; John Steele went to the window; stood with his back to it. A short time passed; the military man puffed more quickly. It seemed the irony of fate, or friendship, that now that he was just beginning to get better acquainted with Steele the latter should inconsistently determine to leave London.

"Anything I can do for you when you're away?" began Captain Forsythe. "Command me, if there is. Needn't say--"

"There's only one thing," John Steele looked at him; his voice was steady, quiet. "And we've already spoken about that. You will let me know if Ronsdale doesn't keep to the letter of the condition?"

"Very well." Captain Forsythe's expression changed slightly, but the other did not appear to notice. "Although I don't imagine the contingency will arise," he added vaguely, looking at his cigar rather than John Steele.

"Nevertheless I shall leave with you certified copies of all the papers," said Steele in a short matter-of-fact tone. "These, together with the one you furnished me, are absolutely conclusive."

"The one I furnished you!" Captain Forsythe rested his chin on the knob of his stick. "Odd about that, wasn't it?--that the day in the library at Strathorn House, when I was about to tell you how I had better success the second time I visited the landlady, we should have been interrupted. And," looking at the other furtively, "by Jocelyn Wray!" Steele did not answer. "If I had only seen the drift of your inquiries, had detected more than a mere perfunctory interest! With the confession given me on her death-bed by the landlady, that she had testified falsely to protect her good-for-nothing son, and acknowledging that another whom she did not know by name, but whom she described minutely, had entered the house on the fatal night-- with this confession in your hands, a world of trouble might have been saved. As it is," he ended half-ruefully, "you have found me most unlike the proverbial friend in need, who is--"

"A friend, indeed!" said John Steele, placing a hand on the other's shoulder, while a smile, somewhat constrained, lighted his face for a moment. "Who at once rose to the occasion; hastened to London on the receipt of a letter that was surely a test of friendship--"

"Oh, I don't know about that!" quickly. "Test of friendship, indeed!" Captain Forsythe looked slightly embarrassed beneath the keen searching eyes. "Don't think of it, or--Besides," brightening, "I had to come; telegram from Miss Wray, don't you know."

"Miss Wray!" Steele's hand fell suddenly to his side; he looked with abrupt, swift inquiry at the other.

Captain Forsythe bit his lips. "By Jove!--forgot--" he murmured. "Wasn't to say anything about that."

"However, as you have--" John Steele regarded him steadily. "You received a telegram from--"

"At the same time that your letter intercepted me at Brighton."

"Asking you to return to London?"

"Exactly. She--wanted to see me."

"About?" John Steele's eyes asked a question; the other nodded. "Of course; not difficult to understand; her desire to hush up the affair; her fear," with a short laugh, "lest the scandal become known. A guest at Strathorn House had been--"

"I don't think it was for--"

"You found out," shortly, "that she, too, had learned--knew--"

"Yes; she made me aware of that at once when she came to see me with Sir Charles. It was she sent your luggage--"

"Sir Charles? Then he, also?--"

"No. You--you need feel no apprehension on that score." A peculiar expression came into the other's glance. "You see his niece told him it was not her secret; asked him to help her, to trust her. Never was a man more perplexed, but he kept the word he gave her on leaving for London, and forebore to question her. Even when they drove through London in that fog--"

"Yes, yes. I know--"

"You? How--?"

John Steele seemed not to hear. "She saw you that night?"

"She did, alone in the garden of Rosemary Villa. Sir Charles behaved splendidly. 'All right, my dear; some day you'll tell me, perhaps,' he said to her. 'Meanwhile, I'll possess my soul in patience.' So while he smoked in the cab, we talked it over." An instant he regarded John Steele as if inviting him to look behind these mere words; but John Steele's half-averted face appeared set, uncommunicative. Perhaps again he saw the girl as he had last seen her at Strathorn House; her features, alive, alight, with scorn and wounded pride.

"Well?" he said shortly. "And the upshot of it all was--"

"She suggested my going to Lord Ronsdale."

"To invoke his assistance, perhaps!" Steele once more laughed. "As an old friend!" Captain Forsythe started to speak; the other went on: "Well, we'll keep his secret, as long as he keeps his compact."

"But--"

"I promised. What does it matter? Sir Charles may be disappointed at not being able to bring about--But for her sake--that is the main consideration."

"And you, the question of your own innocence--to her?" Forsythe looked at him narrowly, smiled slightly to himself.

"Is--inconsequential! The main point is--the 'Frisco Pet is dead. Gillett won't speak; you won't; Lord Ronsdale can't. Another to whom I am about to tell the story, will, I am sure, be equally silent."

"Another? You don't mean to say you are deliberately going to--" Captain Forsythe frowned; a bell rang.

John Steele smiled. "Can you think of no one to whom I am bound to tell the truth, the whole truth? Who extended me his hand in friendship, invited me to his home? Of course it would be easier to go without speaking; it is rather difficult to own that one has accepted a man's hospitality, stepped beneath his roof and sat at his board, as--not to mince words--an impostor. I could have delegated you--to tell him all; but that wouldn't do. It is probably a part of the old, old debt; but I must meet him face to face; so I have sent for--"

A servant opened the door of the library; Sir Charles Wray walked in.

Below, in the cab, Jocelyn waited; her pale face expressed restlessness; her eyes, deep and shining, were bent on the river, fixed unseeingly on a small boat that struggled, struggled almost in vain, against the current. Then they lowered to something she held in her hand, a bit of crumpled paper. It was John Steele's note to Sir Charles asking him to call; stating nothing beyond a mere perfunctory request to that end, giving no reason for his wish to see him.

Her eyes lingered on the message; beneath the bright golden hair, her brows drew together. The handwriting was in the least unlike his, not quite so bold and firm as that she remembered in one or two messages from him to her-- some time ago. But then he had been ill, Captain Forsythe had told her, and was still, he thought, far from well.

She made a movement; the little fingers crumpled the message; then one of them thrust it within her glove. She continued to sit motionless, how long?

The small boat, with sail at the bow and plodding oar at stern, at length drew out of sight; the paper made itself felt in her warm palm. Why did not her uncle return? He had been gone some time now; what--what could detain him?

"Can you drop in at my chambers for a few minutes?" John Steele had written. "A few minutes;" the blue eyes shone with impatience. He was leaving London, Captain Forsythe had informed her; and, she concluded, he wanted to see her uncle before he left. But not her, no; she had driven there, however, with Sir Charles, on some light pretext--for want of something better to do--to be out in the air--

"I'll wait here in the cab," she had said to her uncle, when he had left it before John Steele's dwelling. "At least," meeting the puzzled gaze that had rested on her more than once lately, "I may, or may not wait. If I get tired--if when you come back, you don't find me, just conclude," capriciously, "I have gone on some little errand of my own. Shopping, perhaps."

"Jocelyn!" he had said, momentarily held by her eyes, her feverish manner. "There is something wrong, isn't there? Hasn't the time come yet, to tell?"

"Something wrong? What nonsense!" she had laughed.

She recalled these words now, found it intolerable to sit still. Abruptly she rose and stepped from the cab.

"My uncle is gone a long while," she said to the man, up behind.

"Oh, no, miss; not so werry!" consulting a watch. "A matter of ten minutes; no more."

No more! She half started to move away; looked toward the house. Brass plates, variously disposed around the entrance and appearing nearly all alike as to form and size, stared at her. One metal sign a shock-headed lad was removing--"John Steele"--she read the plain, modest letters, the inscription, "Barrister" beneath; she caught her breath slightly.

"He certainly is very long," she repeated mechanically.

"Why don't you go in and see wot's detaining of him?" vouchsafed the cabby in amicable fashion as he regarded the hesitating, slender figure. "That's wot my missus allus does, when she thinks the occasion--which I'll not be mentioning--the proper one."

"Third floor to the right, miss!" said the boy, occupied in removing the sign and stepping aside as he spoke, to allow her to pass. "If it's Mr. Steele's office you're looking for! You'll see 'Barrister' in brass letters, as I said to the old gentleman; I haven't got at them yet; to take them down, I mean."

"Thank you," she said irresolutely, and without intending to enter, found herself within the hall. There a narrow stairway lay before her; he pointed to it; with an excess of juvenile solicitude and politeness, boyhood's involuntary tribute to youth and beauty in need of assistance, he told her to go on, "straight up."

And she did, unreasoningly, mechanically; one flight, two flights! The steps were well worn; how many people had walked up and down here carrying burdens with them. Poor people, crime-laden people! Before many doors, she saw other signs, "Barristers." And of that multitude of clients, how many left these offices with heavy hearts! In that dim, vague light of stairway and landings she seemed to feel, to see, a ghostly procession, sad-eyed, weary. But Captain Forsythe had said that John Steele had helped many, many. Her own heart seemed strangely inert, without life; she stood suddenly still, as if asking herself why she was there.

Near his door! About to turn, to retrace her steps--an illogical sequence to the illogical action that had preceded it, she was held to the spot by the door suddenly opening; a man--a servant, broom in hand--who had evidently been engaged in cleaning one of the chambers within, was stepping out! In surprise he regarded her, this unusual type of visitor, simply yet perfectly gowned. A lady, or a girl--patrician, aristocratic to her finger-tips; very fair, striking to look upon! So different from most of the people who came hither to air their troubles, to seek assistance.

"You wished to see Mr. Steele?"

For an instant the servant's words and his direct, almost challenging look held the girl. Usually self-contained as she was, she felt that perhaps he had caught some fleeting expression in her eyes, when at his abrupt appearance she had lifted them with a start from the brass letters. The proud head nodded affirmatively to the inquiry.

"Well, you can be stepping into the library, miss," said the man. "Mr. Steele is engaged just now; but--"

"That is just it," she said, straightening. "My uncle is with him, and I wished to see--"

"If you will walk in," he said. "You can wait here."

Jocelyn on the instant found no reason for refusing; the door closed behind her; she looked around. She stood in a library alone; beyond, in another chamber, she heard voices--her uncle's, John Steele's.

CHAPTER XXIII

PAST AND PRESENT

And yet those tones were not exactly like John Steele's; they sounded familiar, yet different. What made the difference? His recent illness? The character of what he was saying, the fact that he represented himself, not another, in this case? He was speaking quickly, clearly, tersely. Very tersely, thought the girl; not, however, to spare himself; a covert ring of self-scorn precluded that idea.

"Those boxes contained books; yours, Sir Charles!" were the first words the girl caught.

"Mine! Bless my soul!" Her uncle's surprised voice broke in. "You don't mean to tell me that all those volumes I had boxed for Australia and which I thought lost on the Lord Nelson came ashore on your little coral isle?"

Came ashore on his coral isle; the girl caught at the words. Of course he had been saved, he who had saved her from the wild sea; she had realized that after their last meeting at Strathorn House. But how? He had reached an island, then--by what means? Some day her uncle would tell her; she understood now why he had sent for Sir Charles, the motive that had prompted him to an ordeal, not at all easy. She was glad; she would never have told herself, and yet she could realize, divine, the poignant pain this lifting of the curtain, this laying bare the past, must cost him. She, too, seemed to feel a part of that pain; why? It was unaccountable.

"Exactly!" said John Steele succinctly. "And never were angels in disguise more foully welcomed!"

"Bless my soul!" Sir Charles' amazed voice could only repeat. "I remember most of those books well--a brave array; poets, philosophers, lawmakers! Then that accounts for your--! It is like a fairy tale."

"A fairy tale!" Jocelyn Wray gazed around her; at books, books, on every side. She regarded the door leading out; was half-mindful to go; but heard the man-servant in the hall--and lingered.

"Nothing so pleasant, I assure you," John Steele answered Sir Charles shortly. Then with few words he painted a picture uncompromisingly; the girl shrank back; perhaps she wished she had not come. This, truly, was no fairy tale, but a wild, savage drama, primeval, the picture of a soul battling with itself on the little lonely isle. She could see the hot, angry sun, feel its scorching rays, hear the hissing of the waves. All the man's strength for good, for ill, went into the story; the isle became as the pit of Acheron; at first there were no stars overhead. The girl was very pale; she could not have left now; she had never imagined anything like this. She had looked into Greek books, seen pictures of men chained to rocks and struggling against the anger of the gods--but they had appeared the mere fantasies of mythology. The drama of the little coral isle seemed to unfold a new and real vista of life into which she had unconsciously strayed. She hardly breathed; her hand had leaped to her breast; she felt alternately oppressed, thrilled. Her eyes were star-like; but like stars behind mist. Strange! strange!

"When the man woke," he had said, "he cursed the sea for bringing him as he thought nothing. One desire tormented him. It became intolerable. Day after day he went down to the ocean, but the surf only leaped in derision. For the thousandth time he cursed it, the isle to which he was bound. Weeks passed, until, almost mad through the monotony of the long hours, one day he inadvertently picked up a book. The brute convict could just read. Where, how he ever learned, I forget. He began to pick out the words. After that--"

"After that?" The girl had drawn closer; his language was plain, matter-of-fact. The picture that he drew was without color; she, however, saw through a medium of her own. The very landscape changed now, remained no longer the terrible, barren environment. She seemed to hear the singing of the birds, the softer murmur of the waves, the purring of the stream. It was like a mask, one of those poetic interpolations that the olden poets sometimes introduced in their tragedies. John Steele paused. Was it over?--Almost; the coral isle became a study; there was not much more to tell. Through the long months, the long years, the man had fought for knowledge as he had always fought for anything; with all his strength, passion, energy.

"Incredible! By Jove!" she heard Sir Charles' voice, awed and admiring. "I told you, Steele, when you were about to begin, that we people of the antipodes take a man for what he is, not for what he was. But I am glad to have had your confidence and--and--tell me, how did you happen to light on the law, for special study and preparation?"

"You forget that about half your superb library was law-books, Sir Charles. A most comprehensive collection!"

"So they were! But you must have had wonderful aptitude."

"The law--the ramifications it creates for the many, the attendant restraints for the individual--I confess interested me. You can imagine a personal reason or--an abstract one. From the lonely perspective of a tiny coral isle, a system, or systems,--codes of conduct, or morals, built up for the swarming millions, so to speak!--could not but possess fascination for one to whom those millions had become only as the far-away shadows of a dream. You will find a few of those books, minus fly-leaf and book-plate, it shames me to say!--still in my library, and--"

"Bless you; you're welcome to them," hastily. "No wonder that day in my library you spoke as you did about books. 'Gad! it's wonderful! But you say at first you could hardly read? Your life, then, as a boy--pardon me; it's not mere idle curiosity."

"As a boy!" John Steele repeated the words almost mechanically. "My parents died when I was a child; they came of good stock--New England." He uttered the last part of the sentence involuntarily; stopped. "I was bound out, was beaten. I fought, ran away. In lumber camps, the drunken riffraff cursed the new scrub boy; on the Mississippi, the sailors and stevedores kicked him because the mate kicked them. Everywhere it was the same; the boy learned only one thing, to fight. Fight, or be beaten! On the plains, in the mountains, before the fo'castle, it was the same. Fight, or--" he broke off. "It was not a boyhood; it was a contention."

"I believe you." Sir Charles' accents were half-musing. "And if you will pardon me, I'll stake a good deal that you fought straight." He paused. "But to go back to your isle, your magic isle, if you please. You were rescued, and then?"

"In a worldly sense, I prospered; in New Zealand, in Tasmania. Fate, as if to atone for having delayed her favors, now lavished them freely; work became easy; a mine or two that I was lucky enough to locate, yielded, and continues to yield, unexpected returns. Without especially desiring riches, I found myself more than well-to-do."

"And then having fairly, through your own efforts, won a place in the world, having conquered fortune, why did you return to England knowing the risk, that some one of these fellows like Gillett, the police agent, might--"

"Why," said John Steele, "because I wished to sift, to get to the very bottom of this crime for which I was convicted. For all real wrong-doing--resisting officers of the law--offenses against officialdom--I had paid the penalty, in full, I believe. But this other matter--that was different. It weighed on me through those years on the island and afterward. A jury had convicted me wrongfully; but I had to prove it; to satisfy myself, to find out beyond any shadow of a doubt, and--"

"He did." For the first time Captain Forsythe spoke. "Steele has in his possession full proofs of his innocence and I have seen them; they go to show that he suffered through the cowardice of a miserable cad, a titled scoundrel who struck his hand from the gunwale of the boat when the Lord Nelson went down, yes, you told that story in your fevered ramblings, Steele."

"Forsythe!" the other's voice rang out warningly. "Didn't I tell you the part he played was to be forgotten unless--"

"All right, have your way," grudgingly.

"A titled scoundrel! There was only one person of rank on the Lord Nelson besides myself, and--Forsythe"--the old nobleman's voice called out sharply--"you have said too much or too little."

John Steele made a gesture. "I have given my word not to--"

"But I haven't!" said Captain Forsythe. "The confession I procured, and what I subsequently learned, led me directly to--Here is the tale, Sir Charles."

It was over at last; they were gone, Sir Charles and Captain Forsythe; their hand-clasps still lingered in his. That was something, very much, John Steele told himself; but, oddly, with no perceptible thrill of satisfaction. Had he become dead to approval? What did he want? Or what had been wanting? Sir Charles had been affable, gracious; eminently just in his manner. But the old man's sensibilities had been cruelly shocked; Ronsdale, the son of his old friend, a miserable coward who, if the truth were known, would be asked to resign from every club he belonged to! And he, Sir Charles, had desired a closer bond between him and one he loved well, his own niece!

Perhaps John Steele divined why the hearty old man's face had grown so grave. Sir Charles might well experience shame for this retrogression of one of his own class, the broken obligations of nobility; the traditions shattered. But he thanked John Steele in an old-fashioned, courtly way for what he had once done for his niece whose life he had saved. Perhaps it was the reaction in himself; perhaps John Steele merely fancied a distance in the other's very full and punctilious expression of personal indebtedness; his courteous reiteration that he should feel honored by his presence at any and all times at his house!

For a few moments now John Steele remained motionless, listening to their departing footsteps; then turned and gazed around him.

Never had his rooms appeared more cheerless, more barren, more empty. No, not empty; they were filled with memories. Hardly pleasant ones; recollections of struggles, contentions that had led him to--what? His chambers seemed very still; the little street very silent. Time had been when he had not felt its solitude; now he experienced only a sense of irksomeness, isolation. The man squared his shoulders and looked out again from the window toward that small bit of the river he could just discern. Once he had gazed at it when its song seemed to be of the green banks and flowers it had passed by; but that had been on a fairer occasion; at the close of a joyous, spring day. How it came back to him; the solemn court of justice, the beautiful face, an open doorway, with the sunshine golden without and a figure that, ere passing into it, had turned to look back! It was but for an instant, yet again his gaze seemed to leap to that luring light, the passing gleam of her eyes, that had lingered--

That he saw now! or was it a dream? At the threshold near-by, some one looked out; some one as fair, fairer, if that could be, whose cheeks wore the tint of the wild rose.

"Pardon me; I came up to see if my uncle--"

He stared at her, at the beautiful, tremulous lips, the sheen of her hair--

"You!--"

"Yes." She raised a small, gloved hand and swept back a disordered tress.

"Your--your uncle has just gone," he said.

"I know."

"You do?" He knew it was no dream, that the fever had not returned, that she really stood there. Yet it seemed inexplicable.

"I was in the library when they--went out. I had come up to see--I was with my uncle in the cab--and wondered why he--"

She stopped; he took a quick step toward her. "You were in there, that room, when--"

"Yes," she said, and threw back her head, as if to contradict a sudden mistiness that seemed stupidly sweeping over her gaze. "Why did you not tell me--you did not?--that you were innocent?"

"You were in there?" He did not seem to catch her words. "Heard--heard--?"

A moment they stood looking at each other; suddenly she reached out her hands to him. With a quick exclamation he caught and held them.

But in a moment he let them fall. What had he been about to say, to do, with the fair face, the golden head, so near? He stepped back quickly--madness! Had he not yet learned control? Had the lessons not been severe enough? But he was master of himself now, could look at her coldly. Fortunately she had not guessed, did not know he had almost--She stood near the back of a chair, her face half-averted; perhaps she appeared slightly paler, but he was not sure; it might be only the shadow of the thick golden hair.

"You--are going away?" She was the first to speak. Her voice was, in the least, uncertain.

"To-morrow," without looking at her.

"Where, if I may ask?"

"To my own country."

"America."

"Yes."

"It is very large," irrelevantly. "I remember--of course, you are an American; I--I have hardly realized it; we, we Australians are not so unlike you."

"Perhaps," irrelevantly on his part, "because your country, also, is--"

"Big," said the girl. Her hands moved slightly. "Are--are you going to remain there? In America, I mean?"

He expected to; John Steele spoke in a matter-of-fact tone; he could trust himself now. The interview was just a short, perfunctory one; it would soon be over; this he repeated to himself.

"But--your friends--here?" Her lips half-veiled a tremulous little smile.

"My friends!" Something flashed in his voice, went, leaving him very quiet. "I am afraid I have not made many while in London." Her eyes lifted slightly, fell. "Call it the homing instinct!" he went on with a laugh. "The desire once more to become part and parcel of one's native land; to become a factor, however small, in its activities."

"I don't think you--will be--a small factor," said the girl in a low tone.

He seemed not to hear. "To take up the fight where I left it, when a boy--"

"The fight!" The words had a far-away sound; perhaps she saw once more, in fancy, an island, the island. Life was for strong people, striving people. And he had fought and striven many times; hardest of all, with himself. She stole a glance at his face; he was looking down; the silence lengthened. He waited; she seemed to find nothing else to say. He too did not speak; she found herself walking toward the door.

"Good-by." The scene seemed the replica of a scene somewhere else, sometime before. Ah, in the garden, amid flowers, fragrance. There were no flowers here--

"Good-by." He spoke in a low voice. "As I told Captain Forsythe, you--you need not feel concern about the story ever coming out--"

"Concern? What do you mean?"

"Your telegram to Captain Forsythe, the fear that brought you to London--"

"The--you thought that?"--swiftly.

"What else?"

The indignation in her eyes met the surprise in his.

"Thank you," she said; "thank you for that estimate of me!"

"Miss Wray!" Contrition, doubt, amazement mingled in his tone.

"Good-by," she said coldly.

And suddenly, as one sees through a rift in the clouds the clear light, he understood.

"You will go with me? You!"

"Why, as for that--"

Fleece of gold! Heaven of blue eyes! They were so near!

"And if I did, you who misinterpret motives, would think--"

"What?"

"That I came here to--"

"I should like to think that."

"Well, I came," said the girl, "I don't know why! Unless the boy who was taking down the signs had something to do with it!"

"The--?"

"He said to go 'straight up'!" she laughed.

He laughed, too; all the world seemed laughing. He hardly knew what he said, how she answered; only that she was there, slender, beautiful, as the springtime full of flowers; that a miracle had happened, was happening. The mottled blur in the sky had become a spot of brightness; sunshine filled the room; in a cage above, a tiny feathered creature began to chirp.

"And Sir Charles? Lady Wray?" He spoke quietly, but with wild pulsing of temples, exultant fierce throbbing of heart; he held her from all the world.

"They?" She was silent a moment; then looked up with a touch of her old, bright imperiousness. "My uncle loves me, has never denied me anything, and he will not in this--that is, if I tell him--"

"What?"

Did her lips answer; or was it only in her wilful, smiling eyes that he read what he sought?

"Jocelyn!"

Above the little bird, with a red spot on its breast, bent its bead-like eyes on them; but neither saw, noticed. Besides, it was only a successor to the bird that had once been hers; that had flown like a flashing jewel from her soul to his, in that place, seawashed, remote from the world.

www.ingramcontent.com/pod-product-compliance
Lightning Source LLC
Chambersburg PA
CBHW080908190726
48294CB00008B/2009